DARK
LEGACY

Wendy VanHatten

DocUmeant *Publishing*
244 5th Avenue
Suite G-200
NY, NY 10001
646-233-4366
www.DocUmeantPublishing.com

Dark Legacy

Hidden Truths Series, Vol. 3

Published by
DocUmeant Publishing
244 5th Avenue, Suite G-200
NY, NY 10001

Phone: 646-233-4366

Copy Editor Corie Barloggi

Cover Design and Layout Ginger Marks

DocUmeantDesigns.com

Printed in The United States of America

ISBN13: 978-1-937801-55-7
ISBN10: 1937801551

Dedication

To Rick, who encourages me to keep writing.

Prologue

Almost a year ago these same three men sat around the very same table in the back room of this exact restaurant in San Francisco. This time, their focus is different . . . and much more urgent.

An opened bottle of Napa Cabernet and three partially empty glasses sit in front of them. The first one to speak utters a curse as he raises his glass. "Damn. How did that happen?" He picks up his glass and ponders the dark purple liquid.

Across the small table, a second man raises his glass and offers a toast. "To Reid. May he rest in peace."

Nods all around as glasses clink. Then, the third man proposes another, more chilling toast. "To finding what belongs to us and to eliminating that bitch." More nods.

"Let's get to work."

Chapter 1

Glancing at the ridiculously ornate clock on the bedside table, I notice it's four o'clock in the morning, for Pete's sake. Once again my phone is ringing. If it's like the call I tried to answer just a few minutes ago, no one will be there this time, either.

Shaking my head, I mutter to the sleepy kitty at the foot of my bed, "Four in the morning? Really? I need to get some more sleep if I'm going to continue tackling this house tomorrow . . . today, actually. And, it's not a house. It's a mansion . . . with a heck of a lot of things in it that still require my attention.

"There's just no way I'm answering my phone again, Shadow. Whoever is calling at this time of the morning obviously doesn't know I'm in England or doesn't care what time it is. For all I know, it could be some stupid prank caller or just a wrong number." Nope, I think to myself. Not going to answer it again.

I'm tired and my body is still adjusting from San Francisco time to this time zone. Shadow, my big, fluffy kitty, looks at me and purrs. "I know. I know. The phone woke me, too. But, I am going to ignore it this time." Just like that it stopped. "Good. If it's that important, they will leave a message and I'll retrieve it later, Shadow." He seems to agree as I lay back down in bed, pulling up the covers.

"Damn. It's ringing . . . for the third time. Maybe I shouldn't ignore it. What if it's important? What if it's Clark calling from a different number? Okay, okay, hold on. I'll answer it." Shadow just looks at me as I gesture into the air.

Annoyed, I punch the screen a little harder than I should, and don't even have time to say "Hello" before a throaty, guttural voice spits out at me. "It's not yours. Give it up now before you and others are harmed. Don't make me repeat myself. You won't like it."

Now sitting up, I attempt to respond. But, it's too late. All I hear is silence as the caller is no longer there. Tapping the recent calls icon, it only says unavailable number. Trying to redial doesn't get me anywhere either. The phone sits in my hand.

"Shadow, what's the deal?"

Just like that, it rings again, almost causing me to drop the phone like a hot potato. Instead, I gather my wits and my sternest, four a.m. voice, "Don't hang up, you worthless piece of crap. I am in no mood for your games."

"Ummm . . . Marta?"

Chapter 2

"Sam. Is that you? I'm so sorry I snapped at you. I just had a bunch of disturbing phone calls. Well, one where anyone actually said anything. It wasn't pleasant. So, I was in no mood to be nice if he called again. I apologize for biting off your head. What's up? And, you're up early. It must only be five o'clock in Venice."

"Marta, I apologize to you for calling at this uncivilized time and waking you. But, I just had a disturbing phone call myself. It was about you."

"What? What do you mean it was about me?" Now I am wide awake.

"The caller told me he had kidnapped you and that you would die unless I gave him what he wanted. I was kind of groggy, but I'm positive that's what he said. When I asked what he meant, he just said I should know and I better hand it over. I am so glad to hear your voice, especially with all that business a year ago here in Italy. You really are okay, aren't you?"

"Yes, Sam, I'm fine. I'm in England at Reid's estate. Shadow, my kitty, and I just flew in two days ago from San Francisco. We plan on staying here for three weeks to finish organizing everything that hasn't already been claimed. There still might be some artifacts, artwork, antiques, and possibly jewelry here that need to be returned to their rightful owners and I'd like to get that done as soon as I can. I'm also meeting with an agent who deals in mansions like this. This estate needs to be sold as soon as possible too, because I want nothing more to do with this awful place and its former owner. It's like a nightmare . . . the murders, the thefts, and all the deception. My mind still can't comprehend the fact that Reid was my father. What a monster he was. I will always wonder if Grandma knew any of this about him.

"Oh, Sam, I really hope none of his genes were passed down to me. I just couldn't bear it."

"Marta, please don't worry. You aren't the least bit like him. Surely something snapped in him to make him turn into such an evil man. Remember the good times. You grew up with a wonderful lady; your grandma. Keep thinking of her and you'll get through this whole mess. Now, if you're positive you're okay, I'll let you get back to sleep. You're probably still jet-lagged anyway. One last question, though. Do you have any idea what my caller was talking about? Do you know what he wants?"

"Sam, I have no idea. There are so many valuable pieces here in this place, it could be anything. And, I've loaned Grandma's music boxes to museums and most of her jewelry went on loan to museum collections in Venice as well. As you know, I only kept a few pieces that reminded me of her. So, it can't be anything of mine unless the caller doesn't keep up with the news. But, why in the world would he tell you he kidnapped me?"

"I have no idea. By the way, how's the security there? Hopefully, you have more than just an alarm and a couple of locks."

"I sure do. The security here is phenomenal. Cameras everywhere. Double gates with security cameras pointed in all different directions and now they're connected to the police department. Clark was here about three or four weeks ago and saw to it everything was up and running before I arrived. He worked with the local police to make sure I am protected and gave them my phone number. Then, there are the guard dogs. I believe they are both German Shepherds. They alert me whenever anyone arrives and don't give up barking until I give them a signal. They seem to view me as their master now. They don't mind Shadow and, in fact ignore him completely. But, he does not like them at all. Major hissing on his part. It's kind of funny.

"I believe the only other people with the alarm and gate codes are Clark and the housekeeper, Priscilla. She's odd. She tells me she's a housekeeper and a secretary. But, I can't figure her out. She was here when I arrived and she kept watching me with a disapproving stare. I don't like her. Shadow immediately decided he hates her. In fact, tomorrow or the next day I'm going to give her a severance and send her on her way. I don't want her around here anymore.

"So, I'm perfectly safe here. No kidnappings. I'll let you know if I find something out of the ordinary. Clark will be here soon to help me. Come visit before I sell this ginormous place. You would probably appreciate the grandeur of it more than anyone I know. I'm here for about three weeks before Shadow and I head to Venice."

"Thanks for the offer, Marta. I may take you up on it, but I would let you know first. Stay safe, keep an eye on Priscilla. For some odd reason, I too, have a bad feeling about her and I don't even know her."

"Really? You, too? Shadow is usually right about people and she is definitely on his no like list. I think he likes her less than he dislikes dogs. Does that makes any sense? Anyway, thanks for the call. My internal clock is still on San Francisco time, so I think I'll get up and sort through more antiques. I've barely made a dent so far.

"Talk to you later."

Chapter 3

Sitting in the breakfast room, just off of the kitchen, with my early morning coffee and Shadow on my lap, I reflect on everything that's happened in the past several months. "Has it really been a year?"

Reminiscing, I think back. It all started with Grandma dying and uttering words of warning to me on her deathbed. That whole scene is so surreal, even now when I think about it. I still wonder how much she knew and if she would have filled me in on details if she had more time. Her warnings about people stealing things were right on target. Things did get stolen; valuable things. Her warnings about not trusting anyone also came true. But, I have no idea if any of those warnings coincided with the actual events. I mean . . . how could she possibly know what was going to happen?

After her death I discovered plenty of things about my grandma. Funny how I thought I knew everything about her when she was living. Guess not . . .

First, I met with her attorney who read her will to me. I found out she had a small palace in Venice, a grape growing estate in the foothills of the Dolomites in Italy, and a bank account that was staggering. My grandma. Who knew?

After her funeral in Minnesota, I stayed long enough to get all of her things settled, her house sold, and then I headed back home to San Francisco. That's when the boxes arrived . . . from her. Actually, her explicit instructions to her attorney were to have them sent to me after she died. The magnificent items these boxes contained still boggle my mind. And, since she was dead . . . I couldn't ask her about any of them—or even thank her. Her attorney had no idea what the boxes contained so he wasn't of any help, either.

First, there were the two priceless music boxes I later found out had belonged to royalty. Her family's royalty, for goodness sake. On top of that were dozens of pieces of valuable jewelry, all old and quite exquisite—again, from her ancestor's royal family. She also sent her old cookbooks, from her days as a professional pastry chef in Venice, and several journals which I still haven't had time to read. Since I'm headed to Venice for some vacation time once I'm finished here, I plan to read through all of them thoroughly. I'm glad I had them shipped from my home in San Francisco to the small palace in Venice I inherited from Grandma.

I remember sorting through all of her jewelry and those fabulous music boxes, deciding what to do with them, when everything changed again. Strange and downright chilling events seemed to follow my every move. People were murdered for music boxes just like the ones Grandma had. People my grandma knew. Right in San Francisco, where I live.

Police, FBI, and Interpol were all involved. The good news is . . . I met Clark, a retired Marine turned art expert and now great friend. I also traveled to Venice where I met Mario, the grandson of Grandma's chef friend in Venice, and Millie. Dear, sweet Millie. Together we all discovered an honest-to-goodness royal tiara and more treasures in Grandma's palace there. It was unbelievable, to say the least.

Now, I can't wait to see Mario, Sam, and Millie again; this time without the drama and ugliness. It was such fun, exploring my property in Italy with, Lorenzo, the co-owner of my vineyards. Unfortunately, while we were all there some more music boxes turned up and then disappeared and, worse, more people were murdered. It was ugly and downright scary for all of us.

I remember it like it happened yesterday. Those were a terrible couple of weeks. No one knew why the murders or the thefts were happening. No one knew if I was the intended target. No one understood who was orchestrating all of this.

Until, that is, the mastermind behind the whole scheme was killed at my co-owner's vineyards in Italy . . . while we were there. According to Interpol, the man's name was Reid and he had a huge estate located in the countryside close to London. Apparently, he started out years ago as an art dealer, possibly even a respected one. Then, for some reason no one can figure out, he turned into a thief, and then a murderer. Several agencies had been after him for years, connecting him to major art thefts and recent murders all around the world. They would get close and then he would disappear. It seemed like he was always one step ahead of them. Until the day at the villa in the vineyards, when he attempted to sneak in. Thank goodness Franz, Lorenzo's guard, was armed and saw him coming.

This part I remember much too vividly. We were all there. Interpol was notified and arrived to retrieve the body. In order to wrap up all loose ends and to see if they could gain any more connections to the thefts and murders, we were asked to view Reid's body. It was gruesome but a necessary piece to put an end to this bizarre chain of events.

All of us understood what had to be done. We wanted an end to this as much as Interpol did. So, we each took our turn . . . Mario, the grandson of Grandma's friend from Venice; Clark, the art theft investigator; Millie, Grandma's friend now in her 70s or 80s from Venice; Lorenzo, my vineyard co-owner; and me. No one, especially the Interpol agents, figured any of us knew him, but it was a measure they needed to take. They asked me to view him first, as I had Grandma's music boxes and jewelry that seemed to be of special interest to him.

Seeing that dead body was a shock I never want to experience again. Never!

A deep shudder reaches to my core, even now when I think about the coroner lifting the sheet off his face.

My grandma helped raise me because Mom and Dad were always off researching some global event or participating in some university archeological dig. When they were killed in a small plane crash somewhere in the Amazon jungle, Grandma and I became even closer. She came often from Minnesota to visit me when I graduated from college and moved to San Francisco. With her Italian heritage and background, she fit right into the North Beach neighborhood in the city. Smiling now and thinking about her, I loved wandering that area with her and listening as she and the shop owners chatted in fluent Italian.

So, when the coroner lifted the sheet and I saw the body, I almost fainted. I know I screamed. It was a scene that will be forever etched in my mind. The man Interpol knew as Reid, the man lying dead on that gurney, was my father. He even had the birthmark behind his ear that confirmed it for me.

Everything that happened after that was either a whirlwind blur or super slow motion . . . or both. I have trouble remembering.

Learning Reid was an evil man, a murderer, a major art thief, and someone who could have killed me, was disturbing to say the least. More disturbing was the fact that this man was my father. How could he have changed from a respected university professor and history buff into this madman? I still can't think of him as my father . . . he will only be Reid to me. In my mind, my father died a long time ago.

Now, I'm left with cleaning up all the antiques and treasures in this humongous mansion that either legitimately belonged to Reid or that he stole. Clark, my friend, art consultant, retired Marine, and rock to lean on, has been the main reason I'm even getting through all of this. Reid's estate initially contained stolen art, artifacts, jewels, and antiques from dozens of countries, countless museums, hundreds of other collectors, and who knows where else.

Most items have already been returned to their rightful owners. Clark dealt with all of that about a month ago. Still, I have dozens of pieces to double check. Contacting museums and collectors is time consuming. Asking for proof of ownership is another place where Clark and Sam are invaluable. Sam's area of expertise is jewelry and he's been wonderful in tracking down former owners of the pieces of jewelry Reid had displayed. We don't want to assume anything when it comes to these fabulous items.

Mario, in Venice, lends support and his private jet whenever I need to fly from San Francisco to London or Venice. Thank goodness I have all of them because I couldn't function without them.

Things still puzzle me, though. Asking no one in particular, "Why didn't Grandma tell me more about my father? Or, were her deathbed warnings actually about him and I just didn't get it? She had to know my father had a dark side to him, didn't she? Did she know him as Reid or by another name?

"When did he change? Was he always like this and was he so good at hiding it, no one knew? Why didn't I pay closer attention? For that matter, what about my mother? How did she fit into all of this? Worse yet . . . what if I inherited any of his awful traits? I can't even think like that. Sam is right. Something must have snapped in Reid to make him act the way he did.

"Well, Shadow, enough reminiscing. I'll never know the answers to any of these questions anyway. It's time to catalogue some more antiques before Clark gets here tomorrow. I want to be finished with the furniture and have a good start on the remaining art pieces. Then he can help me figure out where the rest of the items belong and whom to contact."

Chapter 4

It's almost noon and I've only made it through half of this room; although it is a big room. It's huge, in fact. I've made notes on my spreadsheet, hoping the descriptions and markings will help. I'm trying to research to make sure I have everything correct. Muttering to myself, "Is this table Louis XIV, Louis XV, or Louis XVI? Is there another Louis? Do the markings on this crystal statue mean it's Lalique? And, what about these large Grecian looking statues? I mean, who puts statues like this in their den?

"He must have had these glass cases specifically built for each trinket, vase, or statue. They seem to highlight each piece with just the right amount of light. It's amazing, really."

It's a big job but I don't want to sell something that actually belongs to a museum or to a collector. "I have to assume the rest of these pieces weren't stolen as Clark didn't mark them. But, without him here, how am I going to know for sure, Shadow?" Putting down my tablet computer, I sit down and he jumps onto my lap.

Then, he looks at me and purrs as I rub his ears with one hand and touch the gold coin I wear around my neck with my other hand. When Grandma left me a box full of jewelry, I kept some pieces and shared the rest with a museum in Venice. Much of it was too gaudy for my taste, even though it was exquisite. And, there was no sense leaving it in a safe, hidden away, where others couldn't enjoy it. Since it probably originated with my great-grand-mother's royal family line somewhere in Austria or Italy, it seemed only right to let a museum display it. The museum is thrilled to have it on loan.

A few pieces I kept to wear and to remind me of Grandma. When Sam appraised it all, he discovered this gold coin in the bottom of the box and fashioned it into a necklace for me. Wearing it all the time, I feel like Grandma is close to me. As I touch it now, Shadow fluffs up, hisses, leaps off my lap, and dives under the sofa. "What's the deal? What did you hear, Shadow?"

Standing up and turning around I'm face to face with Priscilla. "Damn, Priscilla. Don't do that. You scared me. I wish you would say something or ring the doorbell or at least let me know you're on the premises instead of sneaking up on me."

"Sorry. I'm used to coming and going whenever I please." She doesn't sound sorry at all.

"I know. But, it bugs me the way you come and go now that this place belongs to me."

"I don't think of it as yours. It belongs to Mr. Reid. He lets me come and go."

Taking a deep breath and sighing, I look her in the face. "Reid is dead and he's not coming back. This is my place now. In fact, we need to have a conversation about that. I'm not sure I need your services any longer. We would both be better off if we had an amiable separation. I'm prepared to offer you a generous severance. Let's talk about that this afternoon and I'll have my attorney draw up an agreement. Okay?"

"I'm not sure you understand all the complicated intricacies of this estate. I've been here for over 20 years. You need me. You can't make me leave. I work for Mr. Reid." Crossing her arms, she stands her ground. She's several inches shorter than me, which makes her about five feet tall. But, whenever she talks to me she puffs up like Shadow does when he sees the dogs. If she wasn't so annoying, her stance would be comical.

"Whoa. Let's not get ahead of ourselves. I'll have my attorney stop over and we can all talk about this. For now, why are you here today? Did you have something that needs to be done or are you here to help me with determining where all these items belong?"

Waving her arms as if to encompass the entire room, vehemently Priscilla declares, "Everything belongs to Mr. Reid. It's all his and you have no right to give it away." Her face reddens as her breathing becomes louder. I think she's around 65 years old but right now she looks much older. Hopefully, she won't have a stroke right here on the pristine beige rug or over on the polished wooden floor. That would be messy.

"Take it easy, Priscilla. Let's not talk about this now. Since it's almost noon, why don't we sit down and have lunch. I don't want to upset you. Okay?" The last thing I want to do is have lunch with this spooky lady, but I need to get her mind off of Reid. I'll remember to make a call to my attorney as soon as I'm alone. Motioning her to lead the way to the humongous, state-of-the-art kitchen I glance back at the sofa where Shadow is hiding. Apparently, he's still under it. He really doesn't like her and I couldn't agree with him more.

Chapter 5

Priscilla quickly finishes her lunch and announces she has work to do. "I'm working on Mr. Reid's files so don't bother me. You probably wouldn't understand them anyway." With that, she heads out of the kitchen and up the grand staircase to the office.

"Good riddance," I mutter under my breath as Shadow cautiously makes an appearance in the kitchen. Picking him up and then setting him down by his food bowl, I grab my phone to call my attorney. I would like to get this over with as soon as possible. "Shadow, that woman is completely weird and I'm beginning to think a little unbalanced. Does she really think Reid is still alive?"

Ending the call with my attorney, I mutter to myself or to Shadow who is by now grooming his paws after his lunch. "Darn. I really hoped we could finish this today. He can't come here but will email me a severance agreement by this evening. I can have her sign it and get it back to him. I guess I'll have to put up with her at least another day. In the meantime, I need to get back to cataloging antiques if I'm ever going to make it through all of this stuff."

About three hours later, I'm feeling pleased with myself as I've completed inventorying this entire room. Every item of furniture, every cigar box, every piece of crystal, every lamp, every knick knack, and every statue is now listed on my spreadsheet ready for Clark to look it over. I'm hoping these can all be sold by the auction house and I won't have to deal with them. Whew. This is a big deal. I think about congratulating myself, when I realize there are at least seven or eight more rooms that need to be finished, too. Granted, some aren't quite as large. Most don't have wall to wall antiques. But, still, they have so much in them. Yikes. I need to stay focused as Clark will be here before I know it.

Touching my gold coin, a strange sensation comes over me. "That smell. Where have I smelled that before? One of the last cigar boxes I opened had that same smell, but it was faint. What is it?" I don't have time to think any more about it as fur briefly brushes my leg. I look down.

Practically flying, back claws scratching as they try to gain traction on the wooden floor, Shadow zooms past me, and dives behind an overstuffed chair. "What got into you?" Turning around I see Priscilla standing in the doorway, holding a cane above her head.

"Priscilla, what on earth are you doing with that cane? Please put it down."

Scowling, Priscilla looks around, still holding the cane.

"Priscilla, put it down, please. Now."

Startled, she looks directly at me. "I thought I heard someone down here and I came to inspect. Who is here besides you?"

"No one, Priscilla. It's just Shadow and me. Are you finished working for the day? Are you leaving?" Hoping this is the case, I smile at her. Maybe I can relax again.

"Yes. I'm going home. Mr. Reid will be pleased with what I've accomplished. I took a call from Mr. Mark and he wants you to know he'll be here tomorrow to talk to you."

"What? Who is Mr. Mark and what does he want to talk about? And, why didn't he call me?"

Not answering any of my questions, Priscilla continues. "He said to tell you he has information about your grandma's jewelry. He said that would make sense to you. I'm leaving now." Placing the cane on the table in the foyer, Priscilla puts on her coat and opens the front door. "He said you know him." With that, Priscilla firmly closes the door behind her.

I'm left talking to an empty space. "Who? What information? What's going on?"

Have I fallen down the rabbit hole and am I talking to the white rabbit or is Priscilla the strangest woman I've ever met?

"Shadow, I need to call Clark."

Chapter 6

Hanging up from talking to Clark, I feel a little better. Yet, at the same time, I'm sad and I'm confused. Clark is tied up and won't be here until next week. That gives me more time to get everything ready for him, but I was really looking forward to seeing him again. It's been almost a month since we've been together and I miss him more than I thought I would. After a disastrous first marriage many, many years ago I never thought I would want to spend a great deal of time with another man. Clark is different. Plus, Shadow likes him.

Both Clark and I are confused about this Mr. Mark person. Clark wonders if Mr. Mark could be the same Special Agent Mark Smith from the San Francisco Police Department who helped me with my music boxes shortly after Grandma died. He will do some investigating to see if his suspicions are confirmed. Priscilla tends to use the term "Mr." in front of names, so I guess it's possible. But, neither of us can figure out what he would be doing here in England. Clark has no knowledge of the San Francisco Police Department investigating anything here and it's more than just a little out of their jurisdiction.

"Shadow, why would Agent Mark call Priscilla anyway? Or, is Priscilla confused? Who knows?"

Since I had an early dinner and I'm tired of cataloging antiques, I think I'll explore some more rooms to see what else is here. "Shadow, let's wander around, check everything out, and count the rooms as I'm sure that's one of the first questions the listing agent will ask me. She's coming tomorrow afternoon and I would like to be able to tell her a little more about this place. Let's start with the downstairs." Shadow looks at me and follows along. He probably thinks there are treats involved.

Starting with the grand foyer, I look all around as a possible buyer would as they enter this mansion. Talking to myself or Shadow, "Okay . . . let's pretend I'm a buyer and I just walked up to the front door. What do I see? First off, the front doors are impressive. While a little imposing, they do fit with the grandeur of this entire estate. If I were a buyer, I could imagine my butler opening the two, dark walnut doors with their heavy, gold handles and ushering my guests into the foyer. I would have to have a butler, wouldn't I?" I smile at the thought.

"My guests would first step onto gleaming, white marble floors and then onto a pale gray, plushy area rug. Although the gold flecked wall paper and small oil paintings are fantastic, their attention would be caught by the sparkling chandelier overhead as it bounces its light off two ornate mirrors. And, this is just the foyer! Whoa.

"Well, Shadow, I guess it's an introduction to what the rest of the house looks like. But, it's still hard for me to call this a house. And, it's hard to believe people actually live in places like this. What on earth does anyone need a place this large for, anyway?" Shadow doesn't seem to care and moves over to another rug to take a nap.

"Okay . . . I will continue without you." I walk through the foyer and continue walking on the same cool, gleaming marble floors that lead me one of three ways. I can go left toward the dens, sitting room, and living room. Or, I can head right toward the main kitchen, breakfast room, pantries, prep kitchen, and dining room. Or, I can go straight ahead up the wide, flowing staircase with its gold flecked banister and handrails.

"What's up with everything gold flecked, anyway? Someone must have liked that. In fact, I wonder if Reid had this built or if he bought it this way." In reality, I don't care.

I've been working in one of the two dens and also in the living room, getting things organized. Now I want to check the other den, with its tall, walnut doors. Those closed doors are just as impressive as the front doors. "Why would someone need two dens? And, why does this one have such massive doors?" Shadow is still in the hallway, so I guess I'm talking to myself again. The first den, where I have been working, is more of a showroom for statues, trinkets, knick-knacks, and one-of-a-kind pieces with its glass cases, lighted shelves, and shiny gold décor. In fact, it almost looks like a display room where you would show off your latest acquisitions. I can just envision Reid using it that way, now that I think about how everything was arranged in there.

"Let's see what's in here." Opening the tall doors with their bronze, lion head handles, that same faint smell from the first den greets me and almost makes me sneeze. "What is that smell?" It's not unpleasant, exactly. I just don't like it. "I'm going to keep these doors open and air out this room. Maybe the smell is lingering from something Reid had or wore. I'd like to get it out of here before the listing agent comes." Turning around I see Shadow sitting in the foyer with his ears back. "You don't like that smell, either, I take it."

Making sure the doors stay open, I enter and lights automatically come on around the room. It's like stepping onto a movie set with everything positioned perfectly. Darker than the den where I've been working, mahogany paneling covers all four walls and heavy green velvet drapes the tall windows. Two walls are lined with mahogany shelves and I sink into the plush, rich brown carpet as I step further into the room. Dark brown leather sofas and chairs welcome any visitor to sit and curl up with the super soft, dark green velvet throws. Looking closer at the fireplace, it appears to be a gas one. "Maybe the smell is coming from there. Who knows how long this room has been closed."

All the rooms downstairs are large. In fact, everything seems to be overstated. This room is no exception.

Looking at some of the books on the shelves, I recognize titles and authors on their faded spines. "Wait a minute. Are these originals?" Almost afraid to touch one, let alone open the cover, I take a Mark Twain book off the shelf. It appears to be old, really old, and genuine, too. But, what do I know? "Another issue for Clark," I mutter to myself and carefully place the book back onto the shelf.

Photographs, in their gold frames, are placed on most shelves amongst the books. Not large and not in the forefront, they almost appear as decorations. Until I take a closer look at some of them . . .

Chills run up my arms and down my spine. Grabbing one off the shelf, I see it's a photo of Grandma and me in San Francisco. "What the hell?" I drop it on the soft carpet as if it's too hot to handle. Looking closer, I see another one is a photo of Grandma and me at a sidewalk café in San Francisco. Another one shows Grandma talking to Enrico, one of the men murdered in San Francisco. Suddenly, I'm furious.

"What is going on? How long has he been following me, sneaking up on me, and taking my picture? And, why? Why Grandma? Was he following her, too? This proves he must have known who I was. But, why?" I'm stomping around the room, getting madder by the second. Glancing back at the other framed photographs, they appear to be people I don't recognize and places he must have traveled. Then, I look more closely at them.

"Wait a minute. Some of these I do recognize as the interiors of museums and their exhibits. Was he scoping out a place before he stole something. Or, was he bragging? I don't like this room anymore. I'm going to keep the doors open and not come back here until Clark arrives. I'm also going to take these photos of Grandma and me. Maybe I should give them to Interpol. If they don't want them, I'm going to burn them."

Quickly exiting the den with its strange and bothersome photos, my phone rings. It's an unlisted number again. Sighing, "I'm really getting tired of these."

$\mathcal{C}$hapter 7

Sternly I answer, "Hello . . . and don't hang up."

"Okay, I won't. Hello. Marta, is that you?"

The voice on the other end is one I think I recognize but can't exactly place. Then, he introduces himself, "Marta, you may not remember me. I am Mark Smith, the agent you worked with, from the San Francisco Police Department."

Exhaling a sigh of relief, "Of course I remember you."

No small talk for him, he gets right to the point. "I'm in London and would like to see you. Would it be okay if I came to your place? I've heard it's quite the mansion."

Taken a little aback by his straightforward manner, I ask him, "Is everything alright? Is there a problem with more of Grandma's music boxes?"

"No. Nothing like that. I just want to see you."

Thinking that's odd, but I agree. "Sure. How about tomorrow morning for coffee? I will give you the address and directions. It's off the main roads and kind of hard to find. You will also need the code to get through the front gate."

"I'll take the code, but I have the address and know how to get there. I'll see you around 10 o'clock tomorrow morning, if that's okay."

"Okay. See you then." I'm still a little puzzled.

Hanging up, I decide it's time to turn in for the night. I'm still catching up on sleep from the time differences and from working nonstop. "Shadow, let's go to bed." He purrs and follows me up the grand staircase to one of the back bedrooms where I'm sleeping. Leaving almost all of the lights on makes me feel better as I make my way down the long hall. I'm not easily spooked, but this huge place tends to give me the creeps. Maybe it's just the man who owned it, maybe it's the sheer size, or maybe my imagination is working overtime.

Turning in for the night, thoughts of San Francisco fill my head. Shadow curls up beside me and soon we're both sound asleep.

Morning sunshine peeks through the clouds and makes its way into my window and, at last, I feel rested. Now that I'm caught up on my sleep, showered, and dressed, I'm ready to start another day of cataloging Reid's things. Plus, it will be interesting to talk to Special Agent Mark and see why he's here. Perhaps he's been in contact with Clark and has something more for me on these antiques. For that matter, I guess Reid could have stolen more from collectors in San Francisco and he has information on that.

As I leave the bedroom, I look for my sidekick before I head to the kitchen. Hmm . . . that's odd. Shadow is nowhere to be found and he's usually rubbing up against my legs and begging for his breakfast by now. Maybe he's already waiting in the kitchen for me. Just then I hear a loud, screeching noise. Who's here? Running down the stairs, following the commotion, I see Priscilla scurrying from out of the kitchen. "Get that animal out of here." She's waving her arms around and pointing toward the kitchen.

"What animal? What do we have in the house?" I hurry toward the kitchen, ready to get rid of whatever critter made it past the dogs and invaded this fortress.

Shadow sits on top of one of the refrigerators, glaring toward Priscilla as she follows me back into the kitchen, his ears flat against his head. She points to him, "He scared me half to death. Mr. Reid doesn't like cats. Not in the house, at least. You'd better get him before Mr. Reid gets to him."

Now I know I've fallen into some time warp. "Priscilla. Calm down. First of all, Reid is no longer here. He's dead. Remember? Second, you know Shadow and he's harmless. And, by the way, what are you doing here? It's barely eight o'clock, and I don't remember you telling me you were coming here this morning."

It's definitely past time I talked to her. I'm not sure I can wait any longer and I need to put a halt to her sneaking in and disturbing everything. But, she's already heading out of the kitchen, paying no attention to me, and on her way to the office to do whatever it is she does. As soon as I make a cup of coffee, feed Shadow who has by now come down off the refrigerator and is purring, and make breakfast, I will go talk to her. "This has to stop. That reminds me, I do need to inspect that office as soon as I can. I'd just as soon she wasn't around when I did, though."

Shadow looks at me as if in agreement.

"I almost forgot. Special Agent Mark is coming by at 10 o'clock. If she is still here, maybe he can get a better read on her. Is she crazy? Or, is she still so devoted to Reid she can't fathom he's no longer living? I've never dealt with anyone like her before. And, it's not that I just don't like her. I really don't know what she's still doing here. I thought she was a housekeeper and going to help me catalog everything. But, she disappears and then reappears. I have no idea what she does, Shadow." Shaking my head, I finish my breakfast and coffee as my phone rings. I see it's a call from Sam.

"Marta, how are you? Do you have a minute?"

"Sam, yes I do. I was just finishing breakfast. What's up?"

"I have some interesting news about your coin. Remember I did some research before I made it into your necklace? Well, a few weeks ago I visited with an Austrian jeweler who works with antique coins and he referred me to a jeweler right here in Venice. Henri, the jeweler here, specializes in Venetian ducats, a coin fashioned after the florin of Florence. I had given him photos of your coin, both sides, and late yesterday his assistant, Pedro, called me with some information. He has been researching your coin and was so excited to tell me what he found.

"As near as Pedro can figure out, yours is a coin that was probably used as a trade coin in Venice or at least in this area.

23

It could date back to the Etruscan time period when gold coins were used in Florence and Genoa as well. Some of those coins had images of Christ. Looking at yours, we both believe it has an image of a Venetian doge, which was more common for this area.

"This is a rare and valuable coin. We're talking extremely rare and quite valuable. Definitely something to keep close to you. A few other ones exist in museums, but that's about it. Neither the jeweler from Austria nor Henri knows why your grandma had it but since your great-grandmother came from royalty, it may have been given to her family as payment for something. Pedro also found some history that indicated many royal families actually had their own coins. If that's the case with yours, it would be exponentially valuable.

"Something else Henri and Pedro discovered. There are those who believe these coins are special; more than their value as an antique or their worth in gold. His family heard stories of these coins 'saving' people from all sorts of horrible accidents. Of course, those legends get handed down about many different items. Still, it's interesting. Don't you agree?"

"Sam, thank you so much. Wow. Valuable, with its own legends, huh? I like knowing more about it, but I just wish Grandma were here to ask how and why she had it. I'll need to thank Henri and Pedro when I get to Venice. And, I'll let you know if it becomes my good luck charm that saves me!"

I start to ask another question as the doorbell rings. It dawns on me I didn't hear the dogs.

"I have to go now, Sam. Special Agent Mark Smith from San Francisco is here to see me and this mansion. I'll call you later with a couple of questions."

"Agent Mark Smith? Wasn't he one of the original detectives working on the stolen music boxes? What's he doing in England? Isn't that a little out of his jurisdiction or is he on vacation? Or, are there more music boxes?"

"I'm really not sure. I have all the same questions. It's kind of odd timing but I'll fill you in after he leaves. Thanks again. Ciao."

$\mathcal{C}$hapter 8

Opening the door, I motion for Special Agent Mark to come inside. "Welcome." Again, I think to myself it's funny the dogs didn't bark.

Smiling at him, I look at his face as he enters. It's interesting to watch the reaction a person has when they see this place for the first time. Even the collectors and museum curators are awestruck at the size and grandeur of the exterior front with its carved columns and stonework as well as the foyer with all its gold and crystal. Others comment on the beauty of the whole estate. The seemingly endless tree lined driveway, the grand fountains surrounded by statues, the color coordinated and manicured gardens, and the expansive lawns can definitely take one's breath away. Most people say something; some are even so impressed they just smile and motion with their arms as they enter.

Special Agent Mark has no reaction as far as I can tell. In fact, I can't tell if he even notices anything about this place. What he does do takes me by complete surprise, though. He takes my hands, pulls me closer to him, and kisses my cheek. Too close, too long, and much too friendly. "Marta, it's so good to see you. How have you been?"

Whoa. This is strange. I've only been around him in a professional manner and don't really know him on a personal level at all. In fact, the last time I saw him was about a year ago in San Francisco when he was investigating some stolen music boxes that may have been connected to my grandma's music boxes.

"Umm. Welcome, Special Agent Mark." I don't know what else to say after that uncomfortable greeting from him. I firmly remove my hands from his and step back as he tries to edge closer to me.

"This estate belonged to a man named Reid, who was my father. You may already know about Reid or have read the Interpol file on him. Only I didn't know him by that name. And, I thought my father was dead. He was killed in Italy. Reid, that is. Not my father . . . well, yes actually my father." I'm rambling. I can hear myself talk and I know I'm not making any sense. Usually, I'm not this taken aback by anyone but Special Agent Mark caught me off guard. Really off guard.

"Please, Marta, call me Mark. No need to be formal here. I feel like we're more than friends after all we went through in San Francisco."

What? What is he talking about? "Sure, Agent Mark. I mean Mark. It just seems like a long time ago. I barely even remember when you and Special Agent Lynne came to my house to investigate the theft of some music boxes that were related to the ones my grandma left me. Speaking of Agent Lynne; how is she? We talked a couple of months ago." Leading him into the kitchen, I'm trying to think of things to say to lessen my feelings that are becoming more and more uncomfortable. Mark follows a little too close to me and I swear he brushed my arm with his hand.

"Ah, I'm sorry to have to tell you this, Marta. But, Lynne died in a tragic accident along Highway One south of San Francisco about two weeks ago. I figured you knew about it."

"I am so sorry, Mark. I have been so busy I haven't even had time to read the papers or listen to the news. You must be devastated. What happened?"

"She drove right off a cliff along a narrow section of highway. Her car wasn't found for several days and she was killed instantly. She left a note at her house. Apparently, it was suicide."

"Suicide? Really? She seemed so balanced and pleasant

whenever I spoke with her. We shared a love of animals and traveling. In fact, she was planning a trip to visit me in Venice sometime later this year I believe. I would have never guessed she would take her own life. Are you sure it was suicide?"

"Marta, let's not talk about Lynne. She's gone. Let's talk about you and what you're going to do with all the magnificent antiques and jewelry here."

I'm pouring coffee and splash a little when he mentions antiques and jewelry. How does he know about the antiques? Why would he mention jewelry? Is that why he came? To talk to me about antiques? Does he want something?

"Mark, I didn't have the chance to ask you what you're doing in England. Are you on vacation or did your job bring you here?" Handing him a cup of coffee, I lead him towards the breakfast room.

Shadow goes scurrying past, fluffed up in his hurry to escape this room where he was watching birds outside. That's odd. Normally, he likes people. Except for Priscilla, that is. People usually comment on his huge, fluffy tail or his tiger striped markings, but Mark didn't even say anything. Maybe he didn't notice him or maybe he doesn't like cats.

I reach the table first, but Mark hurries to pull out my chair and keeps his hand on my back as I sit down. What the hell, I think to myself. I hardly know this guy.

Since he hasn't answered me, I ask again. "I'm sorry. I don't mean to pry, but I am curious what brings you to England. Hopefully, it's for pleasure and not for work. Will you have time to do some sight-seeing? There's so much to do in London, you could spend days there. And, the countryside and all the villages around here offer wonderful history. Cambridge isn't that far away and it's a wonderful city. Do you know how long you will be here?"

I seem to be rambling again.

Mark takes a sip of coffee and looks directly at me, making me uncomfortable. What he says next makes me even more uncomfortable.

Chapter 9

"Marta, I came to England to see you."

Taking a sip of coffee right then, I swallow wrong and start coughing. Mark jumps up and pats me on the back; a little too friendly.

"I'm okay, Mark. I just swallowed wrong. I do that sometimes." Shifting in my seat, I move away from him and his hand that is still rubbing my back. "What do you mean, you came to see me? Surely, you have another reason for being in England. Right? I mean we only met a couple of times in San Francisco. Did you mean you would like me to show you around this area?"

"No, Marta. I feel we really had a special connection when we were together. I just can't quit thinking about you. I enjoy your company and would like to see more of you. On a social level, that is."

Now I'm getting more uneasy feelings. I have no desire to see more of this man. What does he mean, he enjoys my company? I only met him two or three times and those meetings were professional. He's okay but a little too aggressive for my taste. And, I think he's talking about dating. Nope. That's not going to happen.

"Mark, I really don't even know you and I have no time to start seeing or dating anyone. I have some major deadlines coming up and have so much to do with this place as well. If you want me to show you around for a morning or afternoon, I could possibly take some time to do that. But, that's about it. And, I leave here in a few days. So, you see, my time is very limited."

"I would love for you to show me around some day, Marta. That would be fantastic."

Damn! Why did I even mention that? Why didn't I just say I didn't have time? Mentally, I'm berating myself for being nice. Now I'm stuck with him.

"Well, Mark, I only have a few hours that aren't accounted for tomorrow. We could start with lunch and do a short driving trip around this area. I don't have a lot of time to spare, though." Maybe then he will go on his way. I really want him gone.

Just as I'm about to tell him I need to get to work, Priscilla enters as she always does . . . silently. And, as usual, I'm taken aback by her entrance. That woman never makes a sound, I swear.

"Priscilla, I'd like you to meet Special Agent Mark Smith from San Francisco. Mark, this is Priscilla, who used to work for the owner of this place." I motion to Mark as I introduce him. She just nods. Mark tips his head toward her and she nods again as she exits. That is the strangest introduction I have ever seen.

"Mark, I apologize for her. Priscilla was Reid's housekeeper or secretary or something. I'm still not quite sure what she did for him. She is going to be leaving here as I don't need her anymore."

"Really? She's leaving? When?"

Mark's quick questions catch me a little off guard. "I'm not sure exactly when. I'd like it to be sooner rather than later. Why do you ask?"

"No reason. It just seems it would be nice to have someone around who knows this place. How long do you plan on staying here?"

"My plan is to return the rest of the items to their rightful owners first. I'm almost finished with that task and have just a couple more pieces I need to confirm. I've contacted an auction house that deals in antiques and they will sell the rest for me. A listing agent is coming today so I can sell this place. Clark is coming to help me as well."

At the mention of Clark's name, Mark blinks, frowns, and takes on a defensive position. I'm not imagining this . . . his posture changed dramatically.

"Marta, why do you need to have Clark here? I thought he was working with Interpol on some thefts in Dubai. Anyway, I can certainly help you just as well. Why don't you tell Clark he doesn't need to stop what he's doing there? You're in good hands with me. I'm sure we can work through all of your antiques and get along without bothering him. And, do you know when this entire estate will be sold?"

What the hell is going on with Mark? How does he know about antiques, why does he not want Clark here, and why does he care when this place is sold? Now I really want him to leave.

"Mark, I hate to be rude. But, I must get some work finished before the gentleman from one of the museums in Vienna arrives. I can give you a quick tour of this floor but then I need to get to work. Thanks so much for stopping by." Standing up, I lead the way toward the foyer. I have no intention of giving him any type of tour and I just lied about a man from Vienna coming today. It's a good thing he didn't realize that.

Mark follows me, again too close for my comfort level. As we step into the foyer, he reminds me about the driving tour. "Marta, I'll pick you up tomorrow about 11 o'clock. We can have lunch in the village and then you can show me the highlights of the countryside. And, don't forget to call Clark to tell him we can take care of everything without bothering him."

As I turn around to shake his hand, Mark leans in as if to kiss me, catching me off guard once again. At the same moment, Shadow darts between my legs . . . hissing. I move aside to let Shadow scurry past me and Mark is left kissing nothing but air. Whew. That was too close for comfort.

With that, Mark touches my arm, tells me goodbye, says he will see me tomorrow, and exits somewhat hastily.

Bending down to stroke a now calm kitty, "Shadow, you are my hero. What was that man thinking? I have no desire to have him kiss me."

Just as I stand, Priscilla comes down the staircase with her coat in hand. Thank goodness she's leaving.

"Oh dear, did Mr. Mark leave already? I have something for him."

Chapter 10

Looking at her like she's lost her mind, I question Priscilla. "What do you mean? Is he the Mr. Mark you were talking about yesterday? How do you know him, anyway? He's from San Francisco. If it is the same person, and you two know each other, why didn't you say anything when I introduced you?" I think to myself it's odd he didn't say anything either if they really do know each other.

Standing up to her full height and attempting to look disapprovingly at me, she tucks a wayward strand of hair behind her ear, adjusts her glasses, glares at Shadow, and says, "I get around. I've met him before. You should have told me when he was leaving. I could have given him my report." With that, she walks past me, through the foyer.

Not understanding what she's talking about at all, I follow after her. I want her to leave. Yet, I want to know what she means. "Priscilla, wait. What report could you possibly have for Agent Mark? He isn't even here on business. Why would you be doing a report for him? Why wouldn't you mention it in the kitchen?" I am really confused.

"It's none of your business. This is between Mr. Reid and me. I'll have to call Mr. Mark at his hotel." With that, she unlocks the door, opens it, and greets the man standing there. "I'm ready to go now, Mr. Thomas." He takes her arm and leads her to a waiting car.

"Priscilla. Wait. Please tell me what is going on. Do you really know Mark? And, is this man your driver? Does he always wait out here for you?" I have more questions but I'm left speaking to the back of their heads as they walk to the car, get in, and drive away.

The two German Shepherds sit quietly by the front door. "Hi guys. I don't suppose you could tell me what's going on?" They look at me, then at each other, and then back toward the front gate. I wonder why they aren't in the back fenced in area where they usually are during the day. I didn't let them out. Did Priscilla? "Okay, guys, let's go back where you belong." Following me, they both obediently enter their enclosed part of the expansive back yard. "I'll let you both out this evening to do your roaming or guarding or whatever it is you do." They look at me like they understand. I shrug my shoulders. Maybe they do.

Going back inside Shadow greets me with a purr. "I am so confused. It's like one big circus around here. Nothing makes any sense." Looking toward the den with the walnut doors, I see they are closed again. "How did that happen?" I ask no one in particular and no one answers. Opening them, I once again detect the odd smell. "These are definitely going to stay open." Shadow's ears are flat back against his head.

I want to call Clark and fill him in on Special Agent Mark but I have so much to do before the listing agent arrives. I definitely need to catalogue a couple more rooms, so I'll call Clark tonight if the time difference isn't too great.

Working through the rest of the morning, grabbing a quick lunch, and moving on to the living room I see it's almost time for the listing agent. Another massive room, the living room has high ceilings, dark furniture, a baby grand piano, a fireplace, and built in shelves. However, the walls are almost all bare. Beige, silk screened wallpaper provided the backdrop for artwork and paintings that used to be hanging here. Thanks to Clark, those have already been returned to their rightful owners. Now, the room almost looks unfinished. I wonder if the remaining paintings and the furniture actually belonged to Reid.

If so, it's more items for the auction house. Which reminds me, I need to call them and confirm their appointment.

Just then I hear dogs barking and the doorbell rings. Standing on the front step is a well-dressed woman who appears to be in her 40s. She's carrying a small leather briefcase and matching purse in the most exquisite eggplant color. This has to be Sandra, the listing agent from the real estate firm, as she looks exactly like the photo she emailed to me. I had given her the front gate code to make it easy for her. Smiling at her, I welcome her inside.

She enters and reacts the way I expected. "I've seen many grand estates throughout my career. This one has to be one of the grandest. Or, at least the entrance is. And the driveway didn't disappoint, either. I can't wait to see the rest of this place. Pardon me. I'm Sandra. We talked on the phone, but I completely forgot my manners from the time I entered the front gate until now. That's unprofessional of me and I apologize.

"You have a wonderful place and I can't wait to see more. We have clients who are looking for an estate that sets them apart from all the others. This one surely would do just that."

We're only in the foyer. I wonder what she'll say when she sees the rest. "Sandra, you have no idea. I'm Marta and I inherited all of this. Yes, we did talk on the phone. Right now I'm in the process of dispersing of all the furniture, antiques, and other furnishings. I have a gentleman from an auction house coming later to talk about when he wants to take everything. I also have some museums interested in some things." I'm not sure what she knows and I don't want to tell her any more than is necessary.

I continue on. "This place is so massive. There's no doubt it would suit your clients. Do you want to take a quick tour first or how would you like to proceed? It's up to you."

"I think a quick tour would be best. I can get a general idea of the rooms, take some notes, and then come back with my team to measure and take photos. Would that be okay? I don't know your schedule, but I would like to get this property description to a couple of my clients who are starting to look. The timing is perfect. We could proceed immediately. Or, is that moving too quickly? What is best for you?"

"Actually, that sounds great Sandra. I, too, would like to work as quickly as we can. I'm due in Venice in a few weeks and would like to be done with this by then. Even if all the paperwork is not wrapped up, at least the process would be started. Shall we start with the kitchen area?"

Sandra nods in agreement and continues to look closely at everything as we leave the foyer and head toward the kitchen. She walks slowly and makes notes, stopping to touch the wallpaper, inspecting a mirror, and stooping down to press her hand into the plush rug. "Are you positive you want to sell this place? Sometimes clients think they do until it gets right down to parting with a place as magnificent as this."

"Absolutely, I want to sell it. There are no wonderful memories for me here and I need to move on with my life." Apparently, Sandra doesn't know the story behind any of this and that's fine. No need to give her all the gory details.

Chapter 11

Slowly we walk toward the kitchen area, stopping briefly so Sandra can take more notes. Seeing the grand layout, state-of-the-art appliances, and clean lines, Sandra exclaims, "This is magnificent. One of my clients is a retired professional chef and he and his wife are looking for a place where they can entertain. He would love this kitchen. Granite and marble counters. Perfect."

"Well, then, Sandra. You need to see what I call the rest of the kitchen wing. We're just getting started."

Waiting for her to continue her notes, I pour us both a cup of coffee. I still haven't become used to drinking tea, even though I'm in England. "Is coffee okay? I don't have very many tea varieties."

"Coffee is fine. I drink either. Thanks. Okay, lead the way. I definitely need to take photos and measurements in here."

Rounding the corner from the main kitchen, we enter a smaller room. Although most people wouldn't call this room small by any means. It's as large, or larger, than many kitchens I've been in. "This is the prep kitchen. It should suit your chef client perfectly."

"Oh my goodness. This is wonderful. So many prep kitchens are tiny with barely enough room for one person. You could easily have three or four in here working at the same time and they still wouldn't get in each other's way.

"Look. There are two small sinks. Smart. I love the way the chopping blocks are built in and have their own garbage bowls connected. And, look at how the knives are stored. Everything is so smartly designed. Do you know who designed this?"

"I have no idea who designed it. But, there are a lot of thoughtful touches throughout the entire place."

"That's okay. I'm sure I can find out. It's been here for about 15 years if I remember correctly. I'm not sure if there was anything here before that or not. Do you know the history of this place or the surrounding area?"

"No, I don't. Like I said, I just inherited it and have no use at all for it. I live in San Francisco and Venice."

"No worries. I'll find out and let you know. It's possible it was designed and built specifically for the owner. Were you closely related?"

At that question, my face must have registered some displeasure. Sandra was quick to notice and apologized. "I'm sorry. I didn't mean to pry. Sometimes we hear a good story about a place that works well when showing it to prospective clients. You can tell me to stop asking questions at any time."

"That's okay. The circumstances around the owner were strange." I think to myself . . . strange is an understatement to say the least. I try to give Sandra some facts without disclosing all the dirty, murderous details. "I found out I was related to him and was his only heir. As far as I know, he lived alone in all this space. I have no need for another place and this really isn't my style anyway. So, I would like to sell it and get on with my life. This has already taken up too much time, with selling off the antiques, furniture, and other pieces."

Nodding as I'm talking, Sandra continues to make notes. We look in both walk-in pantries. One pantry is complete with shelves, where every kitchen staple has its own space, neatly organized and labeled. The other pantry includes mixers, blenders, gadgets, processors, and other small kitchen appliances.

"This next room is definitely a plus for anyone with wine knowledge." I open the door just to the right of one of the pantries and motion for Sandra to enter.

"Whoa. I love wine cellars and this one is spectacular." Sandra rubs her hand over the wooden racks and smiles. "Perfect."

Closing the door, I direct Sandra. "Let's move on to the breakfast room and dining room."

Sandra again follows me, taking even more notes. "Nice sized breakfast room. I like the windows overlooking this part of the grounds and the light coming in is spectacular. Oh, I love the dining room. My goodness it's huge. The table in here must seat at least 20. Right?"

"Actually, I think it seats 30. At least I've counted 30 chairs."

"Are you selling this table and the chairs separately or would you be willing to offer them to the buyer?"

"I hadn't thought about that. If the buyer would like them, I would definitely be willing to offer that. They seem to fit perfectly in this room. What about the four side tables, three buffets, and five china cabinets? It appears to me they are a matched set."

"They do. I would think the buyer would want all of these. Can you ask your auction agent to hold off on the items in here for now? I'm sure he could always sell them at a later date."

"No problem. This is the room where it makes the most sense to keep the furniture with the place. It almost seems like they were commissioned to fit in this room. Look how the wallpaper matches the fronts of the buffets and the interior of the china cabinets."

"I see that. This is exquisite china and crystal. My hobby is antique dinnerware, including china and crystal. May I look at a piece?"

"Please do. I know very little about it as I haven't had time to research it yet. It could be old or it could be a reproduction. I'm not sure. I'd like your opinion since you know more about it than I do."

Sandra carefully opens one of the china cabinets and brings a wine goblet out. Sparkling in the light, it's easy to see this is a fine piece. Reading the name etched in the base of the wine glass, she tells me it is indeed real. Then, she tells me she thinks this glass would cost about $200.

"Seriously?" I have fine crystal at home and in Venice, but . . . seriously? One glass?

"Yes, I'm sure. Are you selling it as well?"

I'm overwhelmed to say the least. There is so much more in this place than I had even realized.

"Well, Sandra. It appears like I have some more major decisions about the items here. I am selling everything as I want nothing from here. It's not mine nor do I have any desire to have any of it." I may have been a little strong in my words as Sandra looks at me with a puzzled look.

Chapter 12

"I'm sorry, Sandra, to come across so strong. It's just so overwhelming, everything that's here. I have absolutely no need for any of it since my grandma left me some pretty amazing furniture and antiques in Venice. Plus, none of this was ever in my family. At least, not that I knew about. So, you see, it has no sentimental value for me, either. I just want to be finished with everything here; the place, antiques, and furnishings. You have a better feel for your clients. Are there things you think I should try to leave and include in the asking price?"

"Marta, I think many pieces may be of interest. Depending on the client, of course. Some already have a great deal of items such as these fine pieces. Others would certainly love to add to their collections. Still others are moving from nice places but smaller than this and might need additional furniture, glassware, and such. Once my team sees everything here, they would also have an idea of what you could include in the asking price. Do you have to let the auction house know today which pieces you want them to sell?"

"Probably not. I was just in a hurry, like I said. Why don't we continue with the rest of the tour and I'll visit with the man from the auction house to see what he has to say. Some items may still need to be returned to museums or other collectors."

"What do you mean, returned to museums? Are some of these pieces on loan from them or from collectors?"

Oh dear. Now I probably need to fill Sandra in on a little more of what's going on here. Where do I start and how much do I tell her?

"Sandra, I should tell you a little more about this place. I have no idea if anything was in the news about the former owner or not."

When Sandra shakes her head and looks at me with a puzzling frown, I have to assume everything about Reid and his actions was kept pretty quiet.

"Here's the brief version. The man who owned this house was, at one time, a legitimate art collector. Apparently, at some point he decided also to steal art and antiques. Again, apparently from museums and collectors all over the world. When I inherited it, I had no idea how large this estate was and no idea about the number of things here. Now, I also have to figure out what is real, what may have been stolen, and what I'm going to do about all of it. So, I am working with an art investigator, a museum curator, and a jeweler to return the appropriate pieces to their rightful owners. What's left will be sold at the auction house.

"You can see why I have no interest in keeping any of it. It doesn't belong to me."

While I'm talking Sandra is nodding. "Marta, I don't believe any of this was in the news anywhere. That's not uncommon around here with wealthy people, though. Most of what they do doesn't make the news. And, it certainly didn't make any news in the real estate world. Other than that this fabulous estate is soon to be on the market. That's what started the buzz with some of our clients. I'm so glad you called our firm."

"Your firm came highly recommended, Sandra. I thank you for your understanding and your efforts to deal with this whole matter promptly."

"Great. Let's get on with the tour. If my clients want to know more about the history of this estate, I guess they'll just have to find it out on their own. My guess is . . . they won't even care once they set foot in here. Lead the way."

Chapter 13

Next to the dining room I point out a small, stunning bathroom. Of course, in reality, nothing can be considered small here. We move on to the other wing of the downstairs.

"Sandra, I've been working in the two dens and living room, cataloging antiques for Clark. He's the art investigator I'm working with. I haven't even looked in the media room or the sitting room yet. We'll take a quick tour of all of these before we head upstairs."

"Sounds good. I have lots of notes that will help my team in preparation for coming back to measure and take photos. I'd like to do that as soon as we can. Would tomorrow be too soon for you?"

"Actually, that would be perfect. I am supposed to give a tour of the countryside to a man visiting from San Francisco and I really would like an excuse to keep that tour as brief as possible. If you came in the morning, I could help you start with whatever you need and only be gone for a short time while you and your team continue to work. Then, I would come back to help you and answer any questions you might have. Would that work?"

"I think that is perfect. Let me text my team and have them clear their day for tomorrow. It will definitely take the three of us all day to measure, make precise notes, and take photos. These days our clients like to see as much as they can before they actually get here."

Walking through the living room and dens, Sandra touches the drapes, bends down to feel the carpets, and runs her hands over the smooth paneling and embossed wallpaper. "Are all the draperies and their fixtures staying?" She has also been looking up at all the chandeliers in the downstairs rooms. "And the chandeliers. Are they staying as well?"

"Yes. All of them stay."

We glance into another powder room. This one is considerably larger and much more elegant than the previous one. Sandra smiles and looks at me. "It never ceases to amaze me the grandeur of some bathrooms. I mean, it's a bathroom. Right?"

Smiling at her and having the same thoughts I ask, "I thought you referred to them differently here in England. Like a loo or something?"

"Yes, that's true. We call it a loo or a lavatory. But, I was raised in the United States so sometimes I use a mish mash of words. Still, whatever you call this one . . . it's a pretty grand place to wash your hands."

"Right. Let's go into the media room." Finishing the media room and the sitting room, we head toward the stairs.

Walking up the grand staircase Sandra and I discuss the best way to stage everything. "Sandra, most of the items will be gone and I'm not sure I want to take the time or effort to have a company come in with furniture to make it look livable or to stage it. What do you do in a case like this?"

"Our clients understand. They're used to grand places with grand furnishings. They will concentrate on things like the condition and quality of the chandeliers, the built in cabinets, kitchen furnishings, rugs, drapes, and such. I wouldn't worry at all about any extra furniture or furnishings. Believe me, they'll understand. In fact, I'm thinking of two clients I will show this to first. I'd bet a lot of money one of those two will make you an offer on the spot. And, I'd bet an equal amount of money the other client will try to up that bid."

"Really? That fast? That would be absolutely fantastic." Motioning for Sandra to follow me, I lead the way down the hall on the second floor. "Let's start with the back bedroom. The one where I'm staying."

"Okay. How many bedrooms are there? And how many baths?"

"Five of each, plus two additional baths. At first, I thought there might be more bedrooms. But, these five are so large they are actually more like private suites. So, I guess there is no need for dozens of bedrooms. Three of the bedrooms have larger en suite baths with separate showers and tubs, walk in closets with built in dressers, and their own sitting rooms. One, which I consider to be the master suite, is considerably larger, with a fire place and a small kitchenette in addition to a larger sitting room. You could almost use that as a private office. The other two bedrooms have smaller baths attached and then have larger ones directly across the hall from them. There is also a large office on this floor, which is the only room I haven't been in. I have no idea what is in it. Guess we'll find out today."

Chapter 14

Finishing the tour of the bedrooms and bathrooms and heading toward the office, Sandra smiles at me. "I think I could get used to having one bedroom of this size. But, I can't even imagine having five. These are some of the most exquisite and elegant bedrooms I've seen in estates. There's just something about these. I can't quite put my finger on it. And, I've seen many, many bedrooms in other homes."

"I know. They almost seem too opulent to me. I mean, who puts chandeliers in bathrooms?"

"Marta, you're right. And . . . not just one chandelier in each bathroom. Two! Talk about overkill."

Just as I'm laughing at Sandra's remark I happen to touch my necklace. My phone rings. Looking at the screen, I see the words 'private number'. Oh dear. Not another call where no one is there.

Answering it on the third ring, I hear the same guttural voice from the other night. "I'm warning you for the last time. Give it up now. I will hurt you and your friends if I have to." Then, silence. There's no point in trying to answer or ask questions. Frustrated, I close my eyes and sigh.

"Marta, what's wrong? You look really upset. Who called? Is there anything I can do?"

"Sandra, I don't know where to start. I have been receiving phone calls where the caller tells me to 'give it up' and I have no idea what he's talking about. I mean, he doesn't even wait for me to ask any questions. I'm confused. And, I'm more than just a little concerned. I'm sorry." With that I head to the office.

Sandra follows. "Marta, there has to be something you can do about the calls. Maybe you should talk to the police and have them trace the calls or something."

"Thanks, Sandra. I plan to do that. I just haven't had time. Tomorrow . . . that will happen tomorrow."

Opening the office door, we see this is no ordinary home office. I'm glad Sandra is here with me. It's like walking into some high tech office suite with a large computer terminal, wall screens, printers, cabinets, and desks. Comfy looking chairs beg one to relax. Two closed doors sit along one wall.

Sandra is the first to speak. "Wow. What do you do with all of this, Marta?"

Still looking around and trying to comprehend everything here, I look at Sandra. "I have no idea. In fact, I had no idea what all was in here. When Clark was here a few weeks ago, he told me it was locked and was going to ask Priscilla for the key. But, he had to leave suddenly to go to Dubai. We both just thought it was Reid's home office and figured Priscilla came here to do whatever it is she does on the computer. There's a whole lot more here than I origi-nally thought, however. Now I really wonder what she does here all day."

Sandra has been walking around and looking at the three big screens on the wall and at the computer screen. "Marta, look here. These large screens show what is happening in three different areas of the estate. I forgot to ask you about a security system, but it appears there's quite a sophisticated one here."

"Yes, there is. There are security cameras all over the entire estate that are connected to the local police. And, you're right. They appear to be connected in here as well. I guess that's a good thing. Right? I need to show all of this to Clark. Maybe he can give me a better perspective of what's going on. In fact, Sandra, I have no idea if your clients would want this to stay or not."

"Marta, it depends on the client. Most are concerned with security and this would definitely appeal to them."

"I forgot, Sandra. There are also two large German Shepherd guard dogs. They respond to me. I'm not sure why, but they seem to obey me. I have no idea whether they should stay or not."

Sandra nods and moves on to examine one of the desks. "I would think the dogs may be an asset, especially living this far out of the way. Privacy is great. But, it's also good to know you're protected in more ways than one."

I begin fiddling with the computer keyboard.

Turning away from one desk, Sandra turns to look at me. "Marta, you're as white as a ghost. Are you okay? What did you find on the computer?"

$\mathcal{C}$hapter 15

Gasping, I grab a chair to sit down before I fall down. "Oh my God. What the hell was he doing with this picture of Grandma and me?"

Sandra rushes to my side. "What is it? What are you talking about?" Once she sees the computer screen saver, she turns to look at me. "This is you, right? Is that woman with you your grandma? I thought you didn't really know the owner of this mansion."

"I didn't. Apparently he knew me better than I thought, though." Now able to breathe a little better, I look more closely at the computer screen. "I remember when this was taken. Grandma, the woman here with me, had come to visit me when I first moved to San Francisco. We were at this restaurant celebrating my move and my first job in the city. I must have been about 23 or so. Why would he keep this all these years? Why did he have it in the first place? I'm confused, Sandra."

Sandra sits down at the keyboard and starts punching the keys.

"What are you doing, Sandra?"

"Just curious. I assume everything is password protected, but I thought I would check for sure. Do you know the passwords? You might be able to find out more if you could see what's here."

"No idea, Sandra. The logical thing to do would be to ask Priscilla, as she is the housekeeper and secretary. But, I doubt she'd tell me anything. She is so devoted to Reid. In fact, she thinks he's still alive. Weird lady. I'll have Clark look at that as well. If he isn't able to access it, he will know someone who can."

Leaving the disturbing images, I decide it's a good time to take a look at the doors on the far wall and see where they lead. "Sandra, I'm going to check out these doors. If there are other rooms here, they would be important for your clients to know about. It appears this large room is well equipped with the latest technology. Maybe the doors lead to a storage room or an equipment room. Every time I think I've seen it all, something else surprises me."

Moving to the first door and opening it, I find another spacious bathroom. "Well, why doesn't that surprise me, Sandra?"

Chuckling, Sandra agrees. "I guess one can never have too many bathrooms. I mean why not have a gorgeous bathroom, complete with paintings and exquisite vases, in your office? Even if the new owners didn't want this large of an office, they could use this room as a media room or upstairs den. They'd have a convenient, awesome bathroom, whatever this room was turned into."

Nodding in agreement, I move to the other door and attempt to turn the knob. It doesn't budge. "I guess this one is locked. Maybe it contains equipment or something since the lock looks substantial. In fact, it doesn't look like any normal knob or lock. Now, I will have to ask Priscilla about this one and how to open it. I'll check around later for a key. There might be one hidden in here somewhere.

"I've probably taken enough of your time, Sandra. Let's head back downstairs and figure out our strategy. Did you receive a text back from your team, yet?"

"Yes, Peter just sent me a text. Tomorrow at eight works for all of us. That way you can get us started and we can finish while you're with your friend. Would that be okay?"

"Perfect, Sandra. Only he's not really a friend. He's actually one of the policemen from San Francisco I met when dealing with some issues there. I think he wants to be more than my friend, but that's not going to happen."

Nodding, Sandra seems to understand I don't want to spend much time with Mark. "Well then . . . let me give you another reason to cut your tour short. You have to meet with us to finalize the contract for selling this mansion. It's quite lengthy. And, we need to get started on this right away." She grins at me as we near the bottom of the staircase.

I like this woman. "Superb idea, Sandra. Thanks for your help."

Sandra gathers her notes in the foyer. "I'll be back in the morning, around eight o'clock, with my team. They are so excited to see this place. And, it was so great to meet you. Thanks for the tour."

Shaking her hand, I reach for the door. At that moment both of the dogs start barking . . . seriously barking.

*C*hapter 16

Sandra and I both jump. Not sure exactly what to do, I tell Sandra to remain in the foyer while I look out to the back lawn from the living room windows. Instead, she follows me to the living room.

I can see the dogs jumping along the far wall of the property, barking. Sandra points to what looks like a shadow of a person on the other side, but it's so far away it's hard to tell exactly what is there.

"Maybe we should head back upstairs to look at the monitors." Sandra follows me.

"Marta, do you know if there is a monitor on the first floor as well?"

"Good question. I believe Clark told me there is one in the prep kitchen. We'll look for that when we go back downstairs."

Entering the office and checking the monitors, neither of us sees anything except the dogs still jumping at the far, back fence. What had looked like a person is no longer there. The dogs don't seem to be as frantic, either. Touching my necklace, my phone rings. Automatically I answer without looking at the screen.

"Those dogs are not going to save you." Then silence.

"Sandra, I am really tired of this guy and—" I'm cut off by my phone ringing again. This time I look at the screen and see it's from the police.

Answering it, I have a lengthy conversation with the policeman. He saw the same thing Sandra and I had seen and assures me the would-be intruder did not enter the grounds. I fill him in on my disturbing phone calls and he tells me a technician will come visit me to see if he can gain anything off my phone. Thanking him, I relate the conversation to Sandra.

"I hope this doesn't hamper the sale at all, Sandra."

"Not at all. If anything, it's a good test to the reliability of the security system. Now, let's look for that monitor in the prep kitchen. It would certainly be easier than running up here. Oh, do you need to do something with the dogs?"

"Yes, I need to talk to them. But, let's find the monitor first."

Sure enough, a security monitor is on the back wall next to another computer screen. This security monitor shows the same thing as the larger one upstairs. Good to know. Sandra makes a note of this while I turn on the other monitor. It boots up quickly with a delicious looking layer cake as the screen saver.

"Sandra, look. This one seems to be where the recipe collection is saved. I would imagine your chef client would love this."

"Fantastic, Marta. We definitely need to make a note of this, too."

Getting ready to leave for the second time, Sandra again thanks me. I follow her out and head to the back lawn where the dogs are now calmly sitting by their gate.

"What's up, guys? I'm glad you alerted everybody, but I wish I knew what you saw. I think I'll let you out to check the entire grounds."

Wagging their tails, they seem to understand what I'm saying. Once the gate is opened, they both bound out and take off towards the wall in the opposite direction. I watch as they run back and forth, stopping every few feet to look up.

That's odd. Is someone over there now? They aren't barking but they are focused on something I can't quite make out. After several minutes they dart off to check the entire grounds. I wonder who taught them to do this. Eventually, they make it back to me, sit down, and give me a look I can only assume it means they are finished. "Do you have any idea what you're looking for or do you just like to run and bark? Now, how about dinner?"

They seem to be in agreement and follow me to the back enclosure again for their dinner. With good manners, they wait until I fill their bowls and motion for them to begin eating.

Looking at the area along the fence where we saw the intruder, I swear I felt someone watching me. But, the dogs continued to eat dinner and aren't barking.

I must be imagining it.

Chapter 17

Shadow greets me as I come back inside and I bend down to scratch his head. "Well, what have you been up to? Want to help me explore the office some more? Let's go back upstairs. I'd really like to know what's behind that locked door inside the office. Oh, I almost forgot. I want to call Clark. I'm not sure what time it is in Dubai, but I need to touch base with him about several things. Come on, Shadow. Help me investigate."

Sandra and I left the main door to the office wing open when we left. We also left lights on but, like most of the rooms here, they must turn off after someone leaves. At least they came back on once Shadow and I stepped foot into the office. Looking around and thinking to myself, I must remember to ask Priscilla about this room. First, I'm going to call Clark. Sitting down in one of the super soft, high backed, leather chairs I place the call. When I reach only his voicemail, I figure he's asleep or working on something where he can't be disturbed. I leave him a message.

"Clark. This is Marta. I just wanted to bring you up to speed on some things here. I met with Sandra, the listing agent, and we explored the mansion some more. Reid had some disturbing photos of Grandma and me. Well, they were disturbing to me. We probably should let Interpol know. They might want to see them for some reason. We made it into the office but there is still one door that is locked. I'm going to try to find a key for it now. Anyway . . . call when you can. See ya in a week."

Searching high and low, I can't find a key anywhere. "This means I'll probably have to ask Priscilla. Or, I guess I could call a locksmith. That might make more sense."

Shadow has jumped up on one of the desks and is looking out the windows. Wandering over to where he's sitting, I have a fantastic view of the expansive back lawn. "Wow. This would be a great place to work." The manicured lawn gives way to forest beyond the high stone wall. If you didn't know there was another fence adjacent to the stone wall, you'd never see it. Looking out another window, I see more well-manicured lawn, a couple of fountains, and the continuance of the stone wall. Fields lay beyond the wall. "This will be a great place for somebody, Shadow. I just hope we can sell it quickly."

Since the computer screen saver gives me the chills, I decide to leave this room and head downstairs for dinner. "First thing tomorrow morning I'm calling a locksmith and a computer technician. I want to get in that room and find out what's on the computers." Shadow leads me to his food bowl.

"Okay. It's dinner time for both of us." Pouring a glass of wine for me, I start a list of things to do. "Darn. I wish I didn't have to show Mark around tomorrow. I really don't have time for that. I wonder if I could cancel. Maybe I should call him and tell him I have appointments tomorrow that can't be changed. No, then he would just postpone the tour. Or, worse yet . . . he'd come and help. I certainly don't want that.

"Shadow, I'm just going to have to take a couple of hours and do this. Like it or not." Shadow apparently doesn't care as he's busy with his dinner.

Once dinner is finished, I check my spreadsheets to see how many rooms I have left. It's not as bad as I thought. I'm completely done downstairs and have lists for Clark, for Sam, and for the man from the auction house. Now, I've started one for Sandra to ask her clients what pieces they would like to remain here. I also have one for Priscilla. Maybe I should change that list to questions for the computer technician and for the locksmith. In fact, maybe I should have all the locks changed. That's probably a good idea. Then, Priscilla can't just come and go as she pleases. "Why didn't I think of that earlier?

"Okay, Shadow. It's time to start on the bedrooms. This should go quickly as they don't seem to have near as much in them as the rooms down here. Let's get a good start before I turn it for the night."

Chapter 18

Making my way through bedroom after bedroom, my spreadsheet is growing. Most of the furniture is similar in the first three bedrooms; beds, dressers, chests, chairs, bedside tables, and dressing tables. I have no idea if any of the pieces are antiques. They're exquisite pieces of furniture, but I just don't know. More questions.

Artwork is arranged throughout this entire floor and again, no idea if it's genuine, if it's been stolen, or what. Knick-knacks sit here and there. I notice several pieces with the distinctive blue and white look of Lladro. Picking one up confirms my assessment. Again . . . stolen or did they belong to Reid? What a mess.

The gigantic, walk-in closets are empty. "Wow, Shadow. This closet is almost big enough to live in. I wonder why a guest bedroom has this large of a closet? Or, maybe it wasn't originally designed as a guest room. I would think these would be selling points. But, I'm not a real estate expert. Let's head to the last empty bedroom before I look more closely at the one where I'm staying."

Bedroom number four is considered the master suite with its fireplace, huge en suite bathroom, separate sitting room, and kitchenette. Walking to the bank of windows I can almost see the entire countryside. "Impressive. Imagine waking up to this view in the mornings. That has to be a selling point as well."

As with the others, the furniture in here is fantastic, the artwork appears to be museum quality, and the small statues and art pieces are pleasingly displayed. "He sure didn't spare any detail, did he? In fact, Shadow, the more I see, the more I wonder if Reid designed this place and how long he lived here. Did he live alone? The bedrooms are pristine and spotless. Yet, there seems to be a lived in quality about all of them. Who lived here with him? Do you suppose Priscilla would tell me? Probably not. And, do I really care, anyway?"

Opening the closet, I see it's as empty as the rest of them. I seem to remember Clark telling me he had Interpol remove all of Reid's belongings. They wanted to check them for something. I can't remember what. That's okay. I don't want any of it.

I finish the notes on my spreadsheet for this bedroom and head down the hall to the one where I'm staying, touching their switches to make sure all the lights will stay on. I touch my necklace just before I hear the dogs barking. It's too dark for me to see outside, so I head to the office to look at the monitors. Again, too dark to see anything. I'm about to call the police when my phone rings and I see it's them calling me.

After a brief conversation, they assure me they will send a patrol out to check around the perimeter of the stone wall, the fence, and property. If they want to talk to me, they'll call and I can let them in the gate.

Since the dogs have quit barking, we all assume it was a critter and not an intruder that caused the ruckus. Still, I am not about to go outside to check. I'm going to head to my bedroom to make sure all of my notes are complete and then I'm calling Clark. As with all the bedrooms, the one I'm staying in is a fantastic room with a decent sized en suite bathroom. Chandeliers in the bathroom and in the bedroom gleam and sparkle. I wonder how they are kept so clean. As with the other bedrooms, the wallpaper is gold flecked, the off-white carpet plush, and linens the softest I have ever felt. The artwork on the walls could be famous or not. I've never heard of the artists and have no idea how to tell the difference. Nothing is ordinary in any of the bedrooms. "Probably good selling points." I mutter to myself.

Settling in bed with Shadow, I call Clark and once more get his voice mail. "That's odd. It's definitely not like him. He must be really busy. I'll leave a brief message and try him again in the morning.

"Hey, it's me. Hope you're working hard. Call me when you can. Bye."

$\mathcal{C}$hapter 19

My alarm goes off early, I take a quick shower, and head to the kitchen. Sandra and her team will be here soon and I want to finalize a plan before I leave with Mark. Shuddering at the thought of spending any time with him, I still wonder if I should cancel.

When my phone rings, I see it's from Sam. "Hello, Sam. How are you this morning?"

"Marta. Are you okay? I had another disturbing phone call about you last night."

"What was it this time? And, yes, I'm okay. There has been some activity causing the dogs to bark, but nothing serious happened. The local police are on top of it. What's the deal?"

"Glad to hear it. This time the caller made reference to your dogs. He said something about the dogs not being able to protect you. Then he said I should tell you to give it up and no one else would be harmed. Any idea what he keeps talking about? He seems to be repeating himself every time he calls."

"None. And, I also had a call referencing the dogs yesterday. I need to think what he said. And, yes, I noticed he has a limited vocabulary when it comes to his phone calls. But, what did he mean by no one else would be harmed? Has someone already been hurt?"

"Not that I know of. Wait. I need to call you back. I'm getting another call from the police here in Venice. I'll call you right back."

With that Sam hangs up and I'm left still deciding what to do about Mark. My phone shows a text from Sandra, telling me they are at the gate and will be at the door momentarily. I decide it's too late to cancel with Mark, so I'll just have to tell him it will be a quick tour.

The dogs alert me that Sandra and her team have arrived at the front door, and when the doorbell rings, I welcome them into the foyer. She introduces me to Peter and Lou, who both smile at me as they take in the opulence of the foyer. Peter, the photographer, is the first to speak. "Wow. Sandra told us this one was grand and she wasn't exaggerating. We've certainly worked with fine estates, but this is amazing. Look at the layout, the way the light comes through, how every crystal of this chandelier sends out dancing prisms, and the whole impression when you see this for the first time. Clients are going to love it. No one has a place like this. Sandra, we'll have this fantastic mansion sold once the client steps foot in this fabulous foyer."

"Peter, you have no idea. I can't wait for you to see the rest." I motion toward the grand staircase.

Lou, the antiques expert, is examining the wallpaper and the chandelier in the foyer and now greets me as well. "Sorry. We don't usually get so wrapped up in what we see that we forget our manners. It's nice to meet you and we definitely can't wait to see the entire place. Peter is a genius with the camera and his photos will be amazing. I'm more the antiques guy. I'd bet this chandelier is antique and I'd also bet it's worth several hundred thousand US dollars. I will use US dollars when appraising, if that's okay. That way, it makes sense to you. Are there more like this one and are they as spectacular?"

Sandra smiles and directs their attention to the tasks at hand. "Okay, guys. We need to stick to our plan. Marta has to leave shortly, so if we have questions we need to ask them now. I think she'll be back by mid-afternoon. Right, Marta?"

"Right. I will definitely be back by two o'clock. Spend as much time here as you need. I'm available to you for questions, although

I may not know the answers. I just inherited this place a few months ago."

"Amazing. Why do you want to sell it? Too big?" Peter has now taken a few more steps past the foyer and is looking at the staircase.

"Peter, it's just not my style. I have no sentimental attachment to it and I already have two places of my own. I just want to sell it and move on." This seems to answer his questions and the three of them get down to business. Peter spreads out his camera cases and readies two cameras. Lou takes out his tablet computer and Sandra directs both of them to start in the foyer making notes and taking photos.

Shadow watches from around a corner. Deciding they're all okay, he makes an appearance. Everyone comments about his looks and he takes the compliments like they were expected.

For the next two hours, Peter takes photos, Lou takes notes, and Sandra measures everything. I try to answer what questions I can. I learn more about the place as they discuss how old some things are, the value of other things, and what potential buyers may want to purchase along with the estate.

"Sandra, it appears you and your team are more than real estate agents. You seem to know so much about antiques and furnishings."

"Marta, when selling an estate such as this we need to know about many things. Our clients expect for us to know everything. And, while we can't possibly know everything . . . we try to know as much as we can that will assist them in making informed decisions. We all have other careers as well. Those careers mesh together and make us a great team."

I nod as my phone rings and I see it's Sam again. "Hi there, Sam. What did the police want?"

"Marta, I'm afraid it's not good news." Sam pauses and I can imagine him rubbing his eyes with his hand.

"Sam. What is it?" I'm concerned.

"Marta. It's Pedro. He was killed yesterday." Sam pauses.

"Oh no. Pedro, the jeweler? What happened, Sam?"

After a big sigh, Sam continues. "His throat was slit. He was found by Henri when he didn't come to work. Marta, it's just like the murders when Reid was alive. Interpol is involved and they're concerned. I can tell."

Chapter 20

After talking some more to Sam, I'm saddened, confused, and angry. To no one in particular I mumble. "Poor Pedro. I didn't even know him and somehow I feel connected to him. He was looking into my coin for Sam. I can't help but wonder if his death is related to all that mess from before. But, it can't be. Reid is dead. Dead. Dead. This has to be a coincidence. I desperately need to talk to Clark."

Telling Sandra I need to make a phone call and that I would be right back, I walk away from where the three of them are discussing crystal.

Once more I get Clark's voice mail. Now, I'm worried. This isn't like him at all. "Hey, Clark. I'm beginning to wonder if something's wrong. Have you talked to Sam? He has some news. Give me a call. Thanks." I think to myself, if I don't hear from him soon, I'm calling his friend in Paris who works for Interpol to see if he can get in touch with him.

When the doorbell rings, once again it dawns on me I didn't hear the dogs bark. Maybe they're busy. Not believing that for a minute, I make a mental note to check on them.

Opening the door, Mark is standing on the doorstep. I didn't realize it was already 11 o'clock.

He steps through the door, grabs my hand, and kisses my cheek before I can get out of his way. Darn.

"Marta, I hope you don't mind that I'm early. I want to spend as much time as I can with you today. We can then plan the rest of our time together later. I see another car in the driveway. Who's here? How long are they going to be here? Are you ready to go? You can ask them to leave now."

What's up with all the questions and the third degree? "Mark, you are early, but I'm almost ready. Don't worry about Sandra, the listing agent, and her team. They have work to do and will work while we're gone. I do need to let you know I don't have as much time, though, as I originally thought. There is just so much to do here before I sell this place."

Mark scowls as he looks past me to where Lou is standing. "It's not a good idea to let them stay here when you're not going to be here. You don't even know them. It would be better if they left. We can wait while they pack up and go."

That's odd. It's not even his house. "Mark, it's okay. I do know them and I trust them. Let me get my jacket and we can go." Walking toward the front closet, Mark is close on my heels and opens the door for me. This guy really annoys me.

"Marta, I insist they go while you're not here. I'm a cop. Remember? This isn't good. They need to leave and come back tomorrow. They need to be gone. Now."

"No, Mark. They're staying. I don't have enough days the way it is. Please don't worry."

I feel like stamping my foot. Damn it. This is my house.

"Marta, I just don't like it. Surely, they can come back another day. If you're uncomfortable asking them to leave, I will. I can go do that right now."

"Mark, no. Let's go and let them do their work."

Sullenly, Mark nods his head. "Please let them know you'll be gone all afternoon."

"Mark, we need to talk about that. I truly only have three or four hours to show you around. That will be enough for you to get a general overview of the countryside and the towns this side of London. I'll show you which highways you can take to get to

Cambridge or to the English Channel or back towards London. You can explore on your own after that. I have work I really need to do."

Mark is looking past me and I feel like I'm talking to a two year old . . . who isn't listening.

As we head out the door, I tell him I want to check on the dogs. He follows me to the back side of the yard. Both dogs are asleep and it registers as odd to me.

Chapter 21

Throughout a pleasant enough lunch and tour of some surrounding small towns, I think to myself this could have been a nice way to spend an afternoon. Except for the fact that Mark was too attentive, I didn't want his undivided attention, and he annoyed me. Why couldn't this be a day spent with Clark? Thinking of Clark, I check my phone to see if I missed a call from him.

Mark notices and asks if I'm expecting a call. "Yes. I left Clark a message about a couple of pieces I want him to look into. I was just checking to see if I missed his call."

Apparently that was the wrong thing to say. Mark pulls the vehicle to the side of the country road and is visibly upset, almost angry. "I told you, you don't need to involve him. I can tell you what you need to know about your antiques. Please don't call him again. It isn't necessary." With that, he pulls back onto the road.

Whew! What was that all about?

Not wanting to upset him anymore, I decide to change the subject. "Mark, it's getting late. I really need to get back to the house. I'm expecting a gentleman from the auction house this afternoon." That was sort of a lie, but I had to say something that might register with him.

"Marta, that upsets me. I so enjoy your company and I want to get to know you better. In fact, I'd really like to take you out on a proper date. We could go somewhere for a whole day or for a weekend before you go to Venice. Let's stop for a drink at a pub before I take you back and we can discuss when and where. Okay?"

"Sure, we can stop for a drink. There's a pub just ahead on the right. I don't mean to upset you, but my life doesn't have time for another man in it right now."

"What do you mean, another man? I hope it isn't Clark. From what I've been told, he's not reliable. You just need to quit thinking about him. I bet he never called you back, did he?"

"Mark, I need to be frank with you. I am engaged to a man in San Francisco. We've been dating for several years now." Wow. Where did that lie come from? I seem to be good at telling lies when I'm talking to Mark.

"What? You are? No one ever mentioned that fact, Marta. Who is he? What's his name? What can you tell me about him?"

Lies on top of lies. Okay, here goes. Whatever it takes to get Mark out of my life. "Mark, my life is private and his life is private. We both work with clients that may know each other and we need to be careful. At the right time, we'll announce our engagement." I'm getting better at weaving this tall tale. I think Mark is buying it but I can't be sure.

We stop at the pub and once again Mark is too close to me and too aggressive with his hands as I slide into a booth. My phone buzzes and I see I've received a text from Sandra. As I check it, Mark asks me who it's from. Since it's none of his business, I ignore him. He isn't happy about that and tries to look over my shoulder.

Finally, I tell him. "It's from Sandra. They had to leave the house as they were called to a meeting at their office. They'll be back in the morning." Thinking it's odd, I have no choice but to deal with it. Mark nods absently as he's reading his own text message. Apparently that one wasn't good news for him as he scowls and shoves his phone back in his pocket. Things are getting stranger by the moment.

"Remember, Mark, I need to get back within the hour. I have the man from the auction house coming."

"Marta, that's fine. I'll get you there in plenty of time." The waitress brings our drinks and Mark smiles, raises his glass, and makes a toast. "Here's to spending more time with you and getting to know you better. Who knows, you may decide to cancel your engagement."

With that, I almost dropped my glass. What the hell? Doesn't he get it?

Chapter 22

Finally, we're on our way back. Mark has been silent for most of the drive and I don't mind. Just before we left the pub, he received another text that seemed to put him in an even worse mood. When I questioned him about the text and asked if everything was alright, he said things were not going as planned. I tried to ask more but it was clear he didn't want to talk about it.

Just as well. I prefer his silence.

Pulling up to the gates, I enter the code and we follow the winding driveway to the front of the house. Mark jumps out and opens the door for me. Conscious of his unwanted attentions, I try to avoid a situation where he could attempt to kiss me. That doesn't stop him from trying, though, and he misses when I duck my head.

"Thanks for a nice afternoon, Mark. Now, I need to go in and get to work. Please enjoy the rest of your stay in England." That should indicate I don't want him coming in with me. I can't assume he got the message, however.

I'm right. He doesn't get it. "Marta, I would love to help you. I'm good at cataloging antiques and jewelry and anything else. I'd be happy to help you. Really, I think I would be good help. It would be great to work together and get to know each other better. We could connect on a deeper level."

Yikes. Standing my ground, I'm firm with him. "Mark, I do not need any more help and I prefer to do this on my own. Everything is almost ready for the auction house, once I hear from Clark on a couple of items. Please, go enjoy the rest of your vacation."

At the mention of Clark's name, Mark is once again visibly upset and lets me know it. "Marta, I'm just as good as Clark is when it comes to helping. I wish you would understand that. What can I do to prove that? In fact, I wouldn't count on him coming to help, if I were you."

"Why? What do you mean?"

"I just mean he has a really heavy case load in Dubai and might not ever return. You and I would make a great team. What do you say?"

"Mark, really it's okay. I'm just about done. Clark already has plans to come here, anyway."

With that, Mark slams my car door. Oops. I shouldn't have mentioned Clark again. "Thanks again for a lovely day, Mark. Now, I must get to work." With that, I run up the front steps, open the front door, and turn to wave to him. "Bye."

Shutting the door before he can come in, I turn the locks and call for Shadow, who has not come running to greet me. "Where are you? I'm home." Still, no kitty. "Shadow, it's me." Lights automatically turn on as I make my way to the kitchen. That's when I see the mess. Not really a mess. More like things out of place. If I hadn't just been organizing everything with Sandra and her team, I might not have noticed.

A hand mixer that should be in the pantry was sitting in the prep kitchen; two drawers were partially open; two chairs from the breakfast room were along the wall and not by the table; Shadow's food bowl was moved. "What's the deal? Did Peter need to move things to take photos?" Maybe.

Shadow comes around the corner, all fluffed up. "What's going on, Shadow? Was somebody here? I thought you liked Sandra, Peter, and Lou." He goes to his food bowl and immediately hisses. "What? What's in your bowl that you don't like?" Picking it

71

up, I smell it. There's an odd smell to it and I don't like it. I need to call Sandra.

She answers on the third ring. "Marta, I will have to call you back. Something terrible has happened to Lou."

"What do you mean?"

Sobbing and talking all at the same time, she's hard to understand. "Marta, I'm at the police station. Lou is dead. I need to call you back."

Chapter 23

"Oh dear, Shadow. I wonder what happened to Lou." Shadow is eating now as I give him a new bowl of food. I replace all the items to their original places and pour a glass of wine. "Shadow, this has been the strangest day. I'm going to relax and call Clark. I really need to hear his voice."

Clark answers on the first ring. "Marta. It's so good to hear from you. I figured you were too busy to give me a call. How are things going?"

"What do you mean, too busy? I've left at least three or four messages for you over the last couple of days, Clark."

"Seriously? I don't show any messages at all on my phone. But, you know what? I had some trouble earlier with my phone and had the hotel IT person look at it. It seems to be working better now. But, he could have deleted the messages and forgot to tell me. I'm sorry. What's been going on?"

"Whew. That makes me feel better. I thought something was wrong. I need to fill you in on a bunch of things here. First, Mr. Mark is Special Agent Mark Smith from San Francisco. He's here on vacation, as near as I can tell. The thing is . . . this is the weird part. He says he came to see me. And, by that . . . he means date me. Can you believe it? I lied and told him I was engaged to a private man in San Francisco. He didn't like that, but I thought maybe he would leave me alone. He tries to kiss me every chance he gets. Shadow doesn't like him at all. He and Priscilla seem to know each other but I'm not sure how. Neither one will tell me."

I stop to take a breath and Clark finally has a place to get a word in.

"Marta, slow down. I'm just as confused as you are. How and why would he even think something like that? Have you heard from him before now?"

"No, Clark, not at all. He came here out of the blue. Oh. Another thing. He is adamant, and I do mean adamant, about me not mentioning you. He doesn't even want me to call you. He gets so upset and angry when I just say your name. I don't get it. He had the nerve to tell me I don't need to involve you in anything to do with the rest of the antiques. He said he was just as good at appraising antiques and would be happy to help me. He also mentioned jewelry and I don't recall mentioning I had jewelry. What's up with that?"

"Marta, please be careful around him. I don't like the sound of any of that. Maybe it's because I'm involved in a serious, high stakes heist here in Dubai and my mind is working overtime. But, I don't think so. Something's off about the whole scene. I wish I could get there before the end of next week. Do you want me to call a friend in London to come stay with you?"

"I think I'm okay. I mean I have all this security. There have been a couple of times the dogs barked at what could have been a person outside the far west fence. The police were on top of it, though. I'll let you know if I'm feeling spooked.

"The real estate team has been here taking photos and measuring everything in preparation for selling this monstrosity. Oh. I almost forgot. I just had a call from Sandra, the lead person. One of the men on her team is dead. I have no idea what happened. She was pretty distraught and was going to call me back. And . . . another thing. Sam called me about someone in Venice being killed. He worked for the jeweler who researched my gold coin from Grandma.

"Clark, what's going on? Why are things happening again? Do you think these recent things are still tied to Reid? I mean we haven't quite finished with everything of his."

"Marta, I have a bad feeling about all of this. I don't like the fact that Mark just showed up. Too coincidental, if you ask me. And, if Shadow doesn't like him . . . well, there you go. I'd trust that cat about people any day. What's up with Priscilla? Have you let her go yet? She's another odd character."

"No, not yet. In fact, I was going to do that today and I haven't seen her yet. She comes and goes at the strangest times. Another thing . . . Mark was overly concerned when I told him I was letting her go. He asked me all sorts of strange questions and even told me I should keep her for a while longer."

"Wait. What did you mean when you said she and Mark knew each other? Are you sure? This sounds suspicious."

"Well, I introduced them the other day when Mark came to the house. They both nodded, didn't say a word, and acted a little uncomfortable. Then, when Priscilla was leaving she told me she had a report for Mr. Mark and would call him at his hotel. That seems like they know each other. Right?"

"Yeah, it does. But, why would that be? I need to do some more investigating on Agent Mark. I wonder if his partner in San Francisco could tell us anything. What was her name?"

"It was Lynne Greystone. Mark told me she ran her car off a cliff along Highway 1 in California a couple of weeks ago. He said it was suicide. I had a couple of conversations with her and she was planning a trip to Italy, including Venice. She certainly didn't seem suicidal to me. But, I guess I didn't know her that well."

"Huh. She seemed pretty stable to me as well. I guess you never know. I think I'll call Mark's supervisor or a friend at the FBI and just do a little snooping. In the meantime, keep an eye on him. Is he coming back to see you or do you know what he's doing in England?"

"I certainly hope not. He didn't say anything when he left and I didn't ask. I was just glad to be away from him."

Shadow is following me upstairs as I talk. I'm carrying my glass of wine and my tablet computer. Lights come on in the hall-way and I switch them so they will all remain on for the evening. Opening the door to the bedroom where I'm staying, I stop quickly and Shadow runs into my leg.

"Um, Clark. I think I have a problem."

$\mathcal{C}$hapter 24

"What is it, Marta? Where are you and what do you mean by a problem?"

By now, I've entered my bedroom suite. Nothing is messed up. Yet, things are out of place. I pay close attention to details, all details. Shadow walks around sniffing as if he were a dog. I'm wandering around opening my dresser drawers, checking my bedside table, looking at my travel jewelry case, and inspecting things in the bathroom as Clark is trying to get my attention over the phone.

"Marta. What is it?"

"Clark, I'm sorry. I just came upstairs with Shadow and walked into my bedroom suite. Things are out of place."

"What do you mean by out of place? Has someone been in your room? Is it trashed? Are they still there? Marta, talk to me. I'm calling the police right now."

"It's weird, Clark. It's not ransacked or anything. But, things have definitely been moved. I travel with a small jewelry case. It doesn't have much in it, but it works for the few pieces I bring along when I travel. It was in a dresser drawer when I left this morning and now it's sitting on top of the dresser."

"Are you sure you put it away before you left? Could Priscilla have been looking through your things? What else has been moved?"

"It could have been Priscilla. I haven't seen her since earlier yesterday. She's odd, but I don't know why she would move my things. Two of my drawers have been rearranged. Things are still neatly folded but not the way I fold things. I'm kind of funny about the way I fold my sweaters and how I put them in a drawer. And, this is definitely not the way I do it.

"I have two magazines and a book on the bedside table. They're still here but in different order than when I left. Two drawers in the bathroom are slightly ajar. It's just odd. Little things. But, definitely not the way I left them."

"You said Shadow is there with you? Is he fluffed up or is he okay?"

"He's okay but he's wandering around, sniffing things. Why?"

"Just curious. He's a good judge of character and of noticing things. Do you think anything is missing? What about your jewelry? Is it all there?"

"Yeah, it's all here. I have two other bracelets and three rings with me. That and the coin necklace I always wear." Touching it now, I get a funny feeling. "That reminds me, I need to tell you about my necklace."

Entering the walk-in closet, I notice something really out of place.

"Sure, Marta. What about your necklace?"

"Clark. Oh my. Someone was in here."

"What? How do you know? What's going on, Marta?"

"All three of my suitcases are on the floor. Open. They were on the shelves, zipped. Now, two are completely open and one is partly open. This didn't happen by accident. Why would Priscilla look in my luggage?"

"That's it. I'm calling Jerry. He lives in London and works with Interpol part time since his retirement from them. He loves a good glass of wine and telling tales. He also has great instincts about people. I'll give him your number and have him call you in the morning."

"Do you really think it's necessary? I mean, I have the alarm and the dogs. This has to be Priscilla snooping around. Don't you think?"

"Honestly, I don't know. Make sure all the alarms are set and I'll talk to you tomorrow. Okay?"

"Okay. Thanks, Clark. I can't wait until you get here. This place is making me crazy."

Chapter 25

"Well, Shadow, this is a fine mess. Priscilla has to go. Tomorrow. Darn it. I forgot to finish telling Clark about my necklace and the call from Sam. I'll call him back in the morning. I've had about all the excitement I need for one day, anyway. Let's get ready for bed.

"Oh, I almost forgot. I also need to check with Sandra about Lou. I wonder what happened to him. Even though I feel bad, I also wonder if there will be a delay selling this place. And, I want to completely check out the office suite. I want no secrets either before I sell or for the buyers afterward. I'll call a locksmith if Priscilla won't give me the key."

Crawling into bed and drifting off to sleep, my dreams take me back in time to a year ago when everything was so unsettled. I must have tossed and turned all night, since it's now morning, I'm awake, and I really don't feel rested. Showered and dressed, I head downstairs to Shadow, who is demanding his breakfast. "Okay. Okay. I'm coming. I guess you didn't have much dinner last night."

I hear Priscilla coming in the front door. At least this time she's making a little noise. She seems to be talking to herself. Taking my cup of coffee, I head out of the kitchen toward the foyer to intercept her before she can go upstairs and close herself in the office.

"Priscilla. Good morning." As I round the corner, I'm stopped in my tracks. Mark is standing there with her. What the hell. "Mark, I don't remember us having another appointment. Priscilla, do you and Mark know each other?"

Puffing up like she does when she's in a confrontational mood, Priscilla tries to look down her nose at me. "We met outside. Mr. Mark is coming to see you and I have work to do." With that, she tries to get past me to the staircase. I'm not about to let her get past me.

"Just a minute, Priscilla. There is no more work for you to do here. This is your last day. I have your severance check and you will need to give me your keys. I also need the key to the locked room in the office suite and any computer passwords you might have. I would appreciate those now. And, I have an agreement from my attorney for you to sign. You may take it to your attorney before you sign it if you want but you will still need to sign both copies saying I gave it to you."

I believe the saying 'madder than a wet hen' fits Priscilla exactly at this moment. She is livid with me, her face is turning red, she's dancing around like a flea, and she turns to Mark. "Mr. Mark, tell her she can't do this. Mr. Reid needs me here. I have work to do. Tell her, please."

Mark intervenes on her behalf. "Marta, don't you think you're being a little harsh with Priscilla? I wouldn't be so hasty, if I were you. She is a nice person who probably has some work to clean up. Why don't you let her stay for a few more weeks? She can help both of us with your antiques. Okay?"

What? Did he really just say that?

"Mark, this is really none of your concern. Priscilla, please give me your keys. Let's go to the office and you can give me the passwords and anything else that's pertinent. Your severance check is quite substantial."

Before we can head up the staircase, I turn to Mark. "Mark, what are you doing here? I have so many appointments today, I really don't have time to chat."

"That's okay, Marta. I came to help you organize your antiques and to talk to the real estate people. I might know some clients for them. You and Priscilla go ahead to the office and I'll wait in the den. Then we can talk about your antiques."

This conversation is getting stranger. I don't want him here, yet I need to get things finalized with Priscilla first. Once she's gone, I can get rid of him. I hope. Priscilla has already started up the stairs and I quickly follow her. I don't want her in that office suite without me. I glance back over my shoulder and Mark is already walking toward the living room. I thought he said he was going to wait in the den.

Priscilla and I enter the office and once again I ask her for her keys. "Priscilla, please don't make this any harder than it has to be. I need your keys. All of them. This house is going to be sold any day now and the new owners will change the locks. So, you see, I need for you to be finished here." I pull the check and papers my attorney emailed to me out of a folder I laid on the desk yesterday. "Please take this check and sign these papers. Like I said, you may take it to your attorney before you sign the final papers. Do you have the keys to this other room, the one that is locked?" I point to the door along the far wall.

Priscilla takes the check, signs the papers without reading them or consulting with her attorney, and glares at me with her hands on her hips and her lips pursed. Her face is getting redder by the second. I'm not sure if she's furious with me for kicking her out, or if she's mad she can no longer come here and work for Reid, or just what her problem is.

"Priscilla, let's part on good terms. Okay? Do you have the keys to this other room and the passwords for the computers?"

With a big sigh, she looks at the locked door and then at the computer monitors. "I have no key to that room. Mr. Reid's assistant does, though. Ask him. The passwords get changed all the time. I have no idea what they are. He has those, too. You'll have to figure it all out now. You'll be sorry you messed with me." With that, she tries to brush past me to the doorway.

"Priscilla, wait. I'm not messing with you. These are the facts; Reid is dead; this place is in the process of being sold. I have no idea about any assistant to Reid, so maybe you could tell me where I could reach him. And, I still need your keys. Please."

With that, she reaches into her purse and hands me a set of keys. "Here, take them. I hope you're happy." She's out the door and down the stairs in a flash. She's quick. Following her, I want to ask if she has a ride. But, as soon as she gets to the front door, it opens and Thomas is standing there smiling. Priscilla flounces through it and Thomas has no choice except to follow her.

I think it's strange I've never even talked to him. And, I do wonder if he waited outside all the time for her. Touching my necklace, it dawns on me I need to ask Mark to leave. Turning around, I see him on the stairs.

Chapter 26

"Mark, where have you been? I thought you were going to wait in the den. Why did you go upstairs? What are you doing?"

"Sorry, Marta. I thought I would come up and see if you needed any help with Priscilla. I guess I must have gotten lost. I wasn't sure where the office is."

Boy, does that sound like a lame excuse. And, I'm not buying it for a minute.

"Mark, I really do not need any help. Since I have several appointments today, I must ask you to leave. I need to work through everything alone. I appreciate your offer, but I have to do this by myself."

"So Clark isn't coming today? I figured he wouldn't make it out of Dubai. He probably won't even make it to help you. But, since I'm here, I can help."

"Mark, Clark will be here by the end of the week. Now, I have work to do and I really do need to be alone to finalize everything. Thanks for the offer."

As usual, whenever I mention Clark's name, Mark stiffens and clenches his fists. Then, he quickly puts a smile on his face. However, one I notice doesn't quite reach his eyes or come across as genuine. "Why don't you let me come back another day to help?

And, let me know what day Clark is coming. I'd like to see him again."

Yeah, right. He sure doesn't act like it.

"Thanks for understanding, Mark. I'll let you know as soon as Clark lets me know. Are you going to be here in England for a while?"

"Yes. I've extended my vacation. I'm enjoying myself so much."

As we're making small talk, I'm leading Mark to the door. I really want to get him out of here and I need to check upstairs to see what he was doing.

"That's great, Mark. Now, again thanks for understanding. I'll be in touch." I open the door and practically force him outside just as my phone rings. "Thanks again, Mark. I'll talk to you later. I need to take this call. It's probably the agent or the auction house. Bye." Firmly, I shut the door and lock it.

I see the call is from Sandra. "Hello, Sandra. What's going on? What happened to Lou?"

"Oh, Marta, it's just terrible. Horrible. I can't believe it. I don't know where to start. I won't let you down. We've already found a short term replacement. But, it's just so unbelievable. Everybody liked Lou. Who would do that?" Sandra is rambling and I want to find out what happened to Lou.

"Sandra, slow down. Are you some place where you can talk?"

"Yes, I'm at the office."

I hear her take a breath, or a sigh, or a sob. I'm not sure which. "Okay. Start at the beginning. All three of you were here when I left. Then, what happened?"

"Right. We were working on measuring rooms, taking photos, and making notes. We had finished the downstairs and were just heading up the stairs when Priscilla came out of the office suite and told us we would have to do the bedrooms first as she was working on some important things in the office. That was fine with us.

"Then, I received a call from the main office telling us an important meeting had been called and we were all to be there in 30 minutes." Sandra takes another big sigh. "We quickly loaded up all our equipment and made it to the office in about 45 minutes.

Only there was no meeting scheduled. I looked at my phone and the call looked like it came from the main office. Only, it didn't."

"What? What do you mean?"

Another big sigh. "Well, the call registered from the main office. Only, they didn't call me. Later, when I told the police that, they checked and found out it was a call that was routed through the main office and it was made to look like it came from there."

"Okay, I'm still confused. Why would someone want you to come to a meeting that wasn't really a meeting?"

"I know. The police are wondering the same thing. Anyway, we get to the office and no meeting. So, we all go our separate ways, agreeing to meet this morning and come back to your place to finish what we had left." Now Sandra is sobbing softly. "That's when—We did. Peter, Lou, and I all went home. Only. Lou's wife came home about an hour after that and found—"

"Sandra, take a breath. What happened?"

"Lou's wife came home at her normal time and found Lou sitting at the kitchen table. He didn't say anything to her. When she came around to the front of him, she noticed he was dead. His throat had been slit. He was dead."

Chapter 27

Sandra is now sobbing much louder. "Oh, Marta. Lou was such a great person. Why would someone do this to him?"

Chills are running up and down my spine. This can't be happening.

"Sandra, what did the police say?"

"They figure Lou probably walked in on a robbery in progress. After all, he was home about an hour earlier than normal."

"Sandra, I am so sorry. Is there anything I can do?"

"No, but thanks anyway. We have to continue to do our work. It's the only way to think of Lou in a positive way. It's what he would have wanted. We won't be there today. But, Peter and I will be there tomorrow with a temporary replacement. His name is Ted and his timing was good. He recently moved from France, where he worked for the same type of firm there. His credentials are fantastic and we really need to keep moving on your place. We're going to do a trial run with Ted and if he works out, he will take Lou's place permanently."

We finish talking and I hang up. Is this too coincidental? Reid is dead. We know that. My phone rings again and I don't recognize the number, even though it's local. When I answer, he introduces himself as Jerry . . . Clark's friend.

We have a great conversation and Jerry tells me he will come out to see me this afternoon and he's planning on staying here. I was going to tell him it isn't necessary until he tells me his hobby is computers. We talk about the unknown passwords and he tells me he loves a challenge like that. I briefly fill him in on Sandra's conversation and he tells me he'll make a couple of calls and be here in an hour instead of later this afternoon.

Shadow has reappeared and is sitting beside me in the breakfast room. "Shadow, we have a new roommate. I hope you like him. Let's go see what we can find in the office."

At the top of the staircase I decide to take a look at the wing with the bedroom where I'm staying. It still bugs me Mark was up here and I didn't know exactly what rooms he was in or what he was doing. All the doors remain closed, even mine. But, I'm almost positive I left mine open this morning as I wasn't sure if Shadow had already gone downstairs. In fact, I know I left it open. Was Mark in my bedroom? I need to check.

Opening the door and looking around, everything seems to be in order. Nothing is sitting out in the open or seems to be disturbed. Still, I know he was here. Somehow I can tell. I leave the door open again and head toward the office suite, Shadow at my side. He'll soon be bored and sit in the window to watch the dogs or birds.

Once again, I know I didn't hear the dogs bark when Priscilla and Mark arrived. Oh well. I don't understand dogs, anyway.

Wandering around the office, I decide to organize, throw out what isn't necessary to keep, and make a pile to ask Clark about. Maybe Jerry can help me with this as well. And, maybe he knows a locksmith for the locked door. Walking over to the door, I try the handle. Still locked.

"Why did I think it would be open?" I mumble to no one.

Working in the office, time flies by and soon I hear the dogs barking and then the doorbell. I had given the front gate code to Jerry, so I figure it's probably him.

I glance at the monitor and see a tall man with short, cropped gray hair standing on the front step with a small piece of luggage. He reminds me of an older version of Clark.

Reaching the door and opening it, I welcome him in. He scolds me, in a nice way.

"Young lady, be careful who you open this door to. I'm sure you looked at the monitor, but I could be anybody." Then he smiles. "I'm Jerry. Nice to meet you. Clark told me you'd open the door so I couldn't help but give my lecture. My daughters never listen either."

I chuckle as he walks in and whistles. "Whoa. This is some place. I should have figured it would be grand, judging by the front gate, driveway, and entrance. I've never understood why people need a house this large, though. Boggles my mind."

"I agree. Wait until you see the rest. You might be more impressed."

Now he chuckles.

$\mathcal{C}$hapter 28

After a brief tour of the downstairs, I show Jerry his room on the second floor. We talk as we walk and if I'm not mistaken, Jerry has not missed a thing. I tell him he can get settled, look around the second floor, and then I'll give him a better tour of the downstairs. After that, I'll fill him in on everything that has been happening.

In the meantime, I'm calling Clark with an update. Once again, I reach his voicemail. "Clark, just thought I would fill you in on things. One of the men cataloging antiques for the agent who is selling this place was killed. The local police think it was a robbery that turned into a murder. I can't help but wonder, though, as his throat was slit. You don't suppose Reid had associates who are still out there, do you?

"Speaking of associates, Priscilla mentioned an assistant to Reid. I'll fill you in on that later. Oh, Jerry is here. Talk to you later."

Just as I'm finishing up the message, Jerry walks into the kitchen. "You're right, Marta. That office suite upstairs is quite the place. I tried my tools on the locked door. It's a lot more compli-cated lock than I first thought, might even be a custom designed one. We should investigate it a little further. Then you can give me the scoop on everything here. I knew this place was here. But, man oh man. This is one over the top mansion. By the way, your cat is a sweetheart. He loves having his ears rubbed."

"You are correct, Jerry. Nothing about this place is small or ordinary. You're also right about Shadow. He loves attention. Once he knows you will pet him, he'll follow you anywhere. Let's have a glass of wine as we explore the office area."

"Fine with me. I never turn down a good glass of wine. Does this place come with a wine cellar, too?"

"It sure does. It's not really a cellar. More like its own room. I'll show it to you now and let you pick the bottle of wine. I'm thinking I don't want to sell the wine with the place. You can help me decide what to do with it." We head to the wine cellar room and Jerry lets out another whistle.

"Wow. This is serious." He's wandering around looking at the collection, turning a bottle to look at a label now and then, and muttering to himself. "Marta, this is one fine collection of wine. You could sell it with the place, but just at first glance you'd need to add a significant amount to the asking price. This is not your ordinary collection. Of course, whoever could afford this place, would probably be willing to purchase the wine at your asking price."

"Good thought. I'll ask Sandra, the agent, about that. I didn't have time before."

Once out of the wine cellar, we open a nice Sancerre, and Jerry makes a toast. "To figuring out the hidden truths of this mansion." We head upstairs to the office suite.

"Okay, Jerry, this is what I call the office suite. I assume Reid conducted his business here. What has Clark told you about him or, better yet, what do you know from Interpol?"

"Marta, I heard the whole ugly story from Clark and then from reading the files at Interpol. I had just retired about the time all of this business with Reid, the murders, and the thefts was happening. Now, I do some consulting for Interpol, the FBI, and for Clark when he needs help. Did he tell you I was his drill instructor in the Marines?"

"Now I get it. Your mannerisms remind me of Clark. Must be the Marine coming out in you."

"Yep. Once a Marine . . . always a Marine.

"But, Marta, I really don't know anything about Reid prior to the Interpol investigations or the circumstances surrounding his death. I do recall the lengthy file mentioning he was associated with some other murders and Clark made reference to those, but I'd have to think about how much I remember. For now, Clark has kept me in the loop, working on finding the rightful owners of all the stolen antiques and other items. And, I still have contacts in the art world that come in handy. Now, your turn."

"Sure, Jerry. Let me start with my family." We sit on comfy chairs in the office and sip our wine as I fill Jerry in on everything in my life up to Reid being killed in Italy. "So, you see, I didn't really know my father, I had no idea he was still alive, and I didn't know who Reid was until I saw the birthmark. It was a major shock to see his face, to put it mildly. I have so many unanswered questions about all of that and I'll probably never know what happened. I'm learning to deal with it. Slowly.

"As you know, Clark has been returning most of the pieces to their original owners. I arrived here at the beginning of the week to catalog the rest, in case we've missed something that was stolen. Everything that remains will be sold at the auction house in London. The man in charge of that is coming tomorrow, I believe. He'll get a good look at what we have left here, take some photos, and set a date for an auction or however he's going to sell the items.

"I guess his people come and move everything out after that. It's kind of like a puzzle, getting all the people to do their part at the right times. Because Sandra, the listing agent, wants to show this estate to clients as soon as possible. Apparently, there are already a couple of clients waiting to see it."

Jerry has been nodding as I'm talking. "Some of that Clark has told me. He also mentioned some recent happenings. Tell me what's going on."

Taking another sip of wine along with a deep breath, I smile. "Let me go back to Italy after Reid was killed." Once more I relate the story for Jerry, starting with the discovery of Reid, his wealth, and this place. I tell him about Sam and Mario and how they fit into the picture, about me loaning the music boxes and jewelry to museums in Italy, and about coming here. Then, I tell him what Sam recently found out about my coin. Since it's kind of hidden in the collar of my sweater, I remove it from around my neck and hand the necklace to Jerry so he can get a better look at it.

Like clockwork, the dogs begin to bark frantically. Looking at the monitors Jerry and I see them run to the east wall and fence, jumping and growling. Jerry sees a figure before I do. "There's someone there and he's running away." He calls the police and reports what he saw. After a conversation, he checks the monitors, switching them so he can see various angles of the back lawn.

"I didn't know you could do that. Wow. We have a view from just about every point you can imagine, including a shot from the roof. I know Clark told me this was state-of-the-art, but this is amazing."

The dogs are still pacing along that section of the wall, but are not nearly as frantic.

"I'm sure there was someone there, Marta. I'm also pretty sure he's gone now. The police are patrolling the area and will keep an eye out. They're also going to put unmarked cars in the area from now on as well.

"Now, where were we?"

Chapter 29

"You know, Jerry. I'm beginning to wonder if there is something to the legend of this coin. It seems like every time I touch it, something happens."

Jerry is examining it and asks, "What do you mean, something happens?"

"It's probably my imagination working overtime after Sam told me about the legend. But, it sure seems like the dogs bark, Priscilla sneaks up on me, or I have an intruder just after I touch it."

"Coins are not my main specialty, but I think Sam's jeweler friend is right about the face on it. This is definitely an image of some important person or ruler. Your grandmother's family may have been more influential in the Venice area than you originally thought and this was their special coin. Sometime we'll have to see if we can find this image anywhere else. That may give us a clue. For now, I'd keep it close to you. It may or may not be warning you, per se. I'm not sure I believe in any of that. At any rate, I agree with Sam. It's valuable, on many levels. Has anyone noticed it or even asked about it?"

"No. Why?"

"Just curious. Pay close attention to anyone who mentions it or asks about it. Okay?"

"You're making me nervous about it, Jerry. Should I keep it out of sight and in my jewelry box?"

"No. I'd wear it if I were you. I wouldn't let it out of your sight. No sense having someone break in, find it in your jewelry box, and take it because they want to melt it down for the gold."

With that, a puzzled look comes over my face. Jerry notices. "What? Did you just remember something, Marta?"

"Okay. Let me continue with the events of this past week. I wonder if I did have a break in here. Where was I?"

Continuing on with my story, I relate the rest of the events to Jerry. I continue on with Venice and end up here with Priscilla, Mark, and what I'm now thinking of as a break in. Leaving nothing out, I tell him about Priscilla's actions today and Mark's unexpected appearances. We talk about Clark's suspicions about Mark, about my uncomfortable feelings when I'm with Mark, and about the fact I don't know how Mark knows the things he knows.

I pour us each another glass of wine as Shadow has made himself comfortable on Jerry's lap.

"Marta, are you talking about the Special Agent Mark from San Francisco, the one mentioned in the Interpol report? What's he doing here, really? And Priscilla. Any idea what her real function was here?"

"None. She wouldn't tell me. When I asked her, all she would say was she was working on reports for Mr. Reid. However, one time she told me she had a report for Mr. Mark. And, yes Agent Mark is the one from San Francisco. Plus, whenever he and Priscilla were in the same room, it was kind of like they knew each other but yet, not really. It was bizarre."

At Jerry's quizzical look, I continue. "Another thing, Shadow does not like Priscilla. He runs and hides when he senses her coming, even though she seems to be able to creep up on me; never making a sound. Whenever she is around, she makes this grand announcement that she is doing something for Mr. Reid. I truly don't think that she thinks he is dead. It's almost like he is gone for a while and will be coming home any day now. And, she wasn't happy about being let go, even though I gave her a nice severance check. In fact, she was furious."

"Do you think she's dangerous?"

"Not really. More of a nuisance."

Shadow has moved off Jerry's lap and is stretched out on the rug.

"I need to start dinner, Jerry. We can look at this room later."

"If you don't mind, why don't I fiddle with the computer and I'll meet you in the kitchen in a little while."

$\mathcal{C}$hapter 30

As I'm putting the finishing touches on dinner and setting the table in the breakfast room, Jerry enters the kitchen. "Wow. Something smells great. I like to cook but this looks as fantastic as it smells. I don't know if Clark told you or not, but my wife died about two years ago. During her illness and now since then, I've turned into a pretty good cook. And, I found I really enjoy it."

"Anytime you want to help me, Jerry, have at it. I love to cook but always love it when someone helps. Especially if that person knows their way around a kitchen. And, no, Clark didn't tell me much about you. I trust his judgment so I didn't ask a bunch of questions. Tell me about your family."

"Like I said, my wife died about two years ago. We have two daughters; one in Paris and one in San Diego where I grew up. We were stationed all over the world when I was active in the Marines, then headquartered here in London with Interpol, and finally retired here. I live alone with my German Shepherd, Husky mix dog, Milo."

"You have a dog? Bring him here. He could stay outside with these two."

"That would be great, if you're sure they won't mind."

"I have no idea. But, we could try it to see how they get along. By the way, did you find anything on the computer?"

I'm pouring our wine and taking dinner out of the oven. "Yes. I did. I'm not sure you're going to like it. I know I don't."

Pausing, I turn to look at him. He's very serious. "What? Were you able to access any data on the computer?"

"Marta, let's eat first. What I found can wait. And, yes I figured out the passwords. I'm not sure if Priscilla was very computer savvy, but she certainly didn't use sophisticated passwords. I would have thought in a high tech office like that, the passwords would be just as high tech. Guess not. Apparently spying and stealing were more Reid's style."

"Don't forget murder."

"Right. Let's eat and you can fill me in on what else you've found here. Have you heard from Clark?"

Jerry is trying to stall me, but what he found can wait. I guess. I show him my spreadsheets of all the furnishings, antiques, and artwork still here. "The ones in red are the ones I need to ask Clark about before I tell the auction house they can have those. The research I've completed on the rest doesn't indicate they were stolen. Those pieces seem to be legitimate. I'm sure the auction house can tell me that as well, but I'd like an idea before they come. That way I know what I'm dealing with. The ones in blue are the ones Sandra wants to offer to the client who purchases this place. If they don't want them, those can be sold as well.

"I did find some disturbing photos of Grandma and me in frames in one of the dens. And, you probably saw the screen saver. I can tell you approximately when all of those were taken, but I don't know why. Reid must have kept tabs on Grandma and on me. Again, no idea why he would do that. It makes me sad to know he knew about me and I had no idea about him. Yet, at the same time, it creeps me out. I mean, he was a murderer and a thief. Not exactly the qualities you want in your father."

"Marta, I can't begin to imagine. I guess you'll have to remember any good times you had with him. Surely, he wasn't always like that. Was he?"

"Not that I remember. As a little girl, I wouldn't like the fact that he and Mom left so much. It seemed like they were always going to far-away places; Egypt for an archeology dig on a tomb,

Turkey for another dig related to some ancient civilization, Antarctica to research something with the oceans. After a while, I lost count.

"What I do remember, though, were the gifts they brought home to me. Not your normal gifts, these would be a vial of sand from Egypt or a feather from an Emperor Penguin. I had the best things for show and tell. Still, it was a strange way to grow up. The best part, though, was Grandma. We were very close because of Mom and Dad always being gone."

"Do you have any idea when he changed from exploring and legitimate treasure hunting to stealing? Does anything ring a bell?"

Sipping my wine, I reflect back to what I can remember. "Not really. They died when I was in junior high. Or, at least that's what I was told. Their plane went down in the jungle near the Amazon River and their bodies were never recovered. Now, I wonder if he parachuted out, if he planned on killing my mother all along, and how he escaped the plane crash.

"I guess I'll never know the real truth. I can speculate all I want, but the bottom line is . . . he turned into a terrible person."

"Marta, let's clean up our dishes and then I want to show you some things I discovered. I need for you to keep an open mind and I need for you to pay close attention to what I'm about to show you. Okay?"

$\mathcal{C}$hapter 31

"Okay, lead the way. I think I'm ready for just about anything."
With our glasses of wine, we head up the stairs and into the office
suite. Shadow follows.

"Marta, you mentioned Mark, an agent with the San
Francisco Police Department. What do you know about him? Tell
me what he looks like."

"Okay. He's about six foot tall, dark wavy hair, broad shoulders like a linebacker, and nice looking but not drop dead handsome. The first time I saw him was when he and his partner came
to my house. They were the agents called to assist me after I had
the first music box appraised in San Francisco. The jeweler who
appraised it was not a legitimate jeweler, even though he had the
credentials. Shortly after he looked at mine, he was killed. It's all
kind of a mess as everyone was trying to figure out if the murders
and thefts of other music boxes were somehow connected to mine.
I had a couple of conversations with both of them during that
time, but nothing after that. Certainly nothing with Special Agent
Mark. Until, that is, he showed up here on my doorstep this week.
Actually, he called first and then showed up. Why?"

Jerry stops at the doorway to the office suite and turns to me.

"I found files of photos on the computer and there appears to
be a man in several of the photos who looks an awful lot like the

one you just described. He's always looking the other way, but you may be able to tell if you've ever seen him before. There are plenty of photos of other people, too. I don't know any of them. But, then again, I wasn't actively on this case. If you recognize any of them, we'll make a note and notify Interpol. I haven't had a chance to completely inspect all of the files. I do need to warn you. There are some photos of you and of an older lady. I assume it's your grandmother. Can you handle this?"

"Why? Are these photos bad? Let's go see."

"Marta, they aren't bad. There are just a lot of them. It appears you were followed for quite some time. As recent as two weeks ago, judging by the dates on this file."

"What?" My voice comes out squeaky. "Who would have done that? Reid has been dead for a lot longer than that. Let me see them."

We enter the suite and sit down at the computer. The screen saver photo of Grandma and me is disturbing, considering it's on Reid's computer. It was taken at a sidewalk café in the North Beach area of San Francisco and we're drinking coffee and chatting with the owner of the restaurant. I'm positive it was when I first moved to San Francisco and I mention the time frame to Jerry.

Jerry looks are me and enters the password. Several icons appear on the screen.

"Okay, Marta, I've looked at the file labeled Marta and the one labeled SF. As soon as I show you the file with your photos in it, we'll go over the rest together. Okay?"

Nodding, I move the mouse over the icon labeled Marta and several additional folders open. They're sorted by years, sort of. Opening each one, there are anywhere from three to ten photos in each folder. Some are with Grandma; some without her. I'm always meeting with or talking to someone. I'm never alone and never in my own home.

Finishing the last folder, I look at Jerry. "Jerry, this last one definitely was two days before I boarded Mario's plane. In it I'm meeting with Bob, a friend of Clark's who is FBI, and his wife Helen. We had lunch at a café in the Presidio and they were filling me in on the security for my home while I am here and in Venice.

I always talk to them before I leave. His wife has a house sitting service and we were finalizing the arrangements.

"Why would someone want this photo? Who is following me? And, why? Why now? Better question . . . why is it here? How did it get here, in this computer?"

"Marta, those are all valid questions and ones for Interpol. Let's look at the folder labeled SF and see if you know any of these people."

Jerry opens that folder and slowly I scroll through about 25 photos. "They are all places I recognize; many are places I frequent. I don't seem to see Grandma or me in any of them, though. Where are the ones with the guy you thought I might know?"

"Look at these two. For some reason, these photos are not as sharp as the rest. But, look at the man in the background in this one and the man standing along the edge of the street in this one. They appear to be the same man. Do you recognize him?"

I would have missed those had Jerry not pointed them out to me. At first glance, it's just a man in a photo that appears to be slightly out of focus. Looking more closely at the man, I nod my head to Jerry. "I sure do. It is Special Agent Mark." I look again. "What's he doing? He almost looks like he's standing guard or watching something or someone, though. And, he doesn't appear to be the main focus of the photo. What do you make of that?"

"Look closer. I wish I could get this magnified. He's with another man, the same one in both photos. Do you know him?"

"No. Not at all. Who is he?"

"I don't know. But, they're definitely together. See how their heads are close together like they're talking about something? I don't know when this was taken, either. I'll send this file to Interpol. I think we should have an agent come out here to investigate further. Would that be okay with you?"

"By all means. Let's do it sooner than later. But wait. Why are there photos of Mark on Reid's computer? Did they know each other or was Reid watching Mark, too?"

"I don't know. Let's look at some more and maybe we'll get a better idea."

$\mathcal{C}$hapter 32

Two hours later, we've looked at all the folders and all the photos and are no closer to figuring out why anything is here.

"Jerry, is that it for the files on this computer?"

"I believe so, for the photos. Or, at least the ones that are easy to access. I'll do more digging because I believe something more is buried here. At first glance, it seems this was just a place for him to store his photos. That in itself is odd. But, then again, he appears to have been an odd guy. However, I'm not buying it. There's more here and I'll find it."

"Okay. I'm going to turn in for the night. I'm not sure my brain can absorb any more. Sandra and her team will be here in the morning to finish their work. If you need anything, please let me know. Good night. "

"Night, Marta. I'm going to fiddle a little more and then turn in as well. See you in the morning. I'll make breakfast."

"Sweet. Thanks."

Heading down the hallway to my room, my phone buzzes and I see I have a text from Sandra. Checking my phone, it appears they can't come until the day after tomorrow. My guess is they don't have that much left to do anyway.

I need to call Clark, but I'll do that in the morning.

"Shadow, we've had a busy day. I'm glad you like Jerry. He has a dog, but he'll stay outside. Let's turn in." Following me like he agrees, we both fall fast asleep and it's morning before I know it. After a relaxing shower, I smell wonderful things coming from downstairs. Shadow has apparently already followed his nose.

"Good morning, Sunshine." Jerry greets me as I enter the kitchen. "This is one begging cat. Did you know he likes pancakes?"

"Right. He likes anything he can get. I see he's already had his breakfast. Or, some of it."

"Yeah. The cat food was okay until I started the pancakes. Then he decided these were better. Beggar." Jerry points a finger at Shadow and sets a plate of fluffy pancakes, a cup of coffee, and a glass of orange juice in front of me.

"Wow. These taste even better than they smell." Taking a bite, I'm in heaven. "These are fantastic. Thanks for making breakfast. By the way, I had a text from Sandra last night. They won't be here until tomorrow. So, we have time to work more in the office. Did you find anything else?"

"I only stayed up a little longer. I thought we could go through more of it this morning and then I'll go pick up Milo and bring him back here. We'll see if he gets along with the two dogs here. His husky-pack mentality might offend the shepherds."

"Sounds like a plan. Let me clean up these dishes and we can head upstairs."

"I thought I would give my contact at Interpol a call as well. No doubt a couple of guys will come here. It's probably best if they aren't here when your listing agent is here, however. It might not look too good. I'll tell them to come later tomorrow if that's okay."

"That's perfect. And, while you're gone, I'll call Clark. I haven't touched base with him for a couple of days. I keep getting his voice mail."

We head upstairs to the office to investigate some more and I point to the computer. "I guess I could have it shipped to Venice or even to San Francisco. What do you think, Jerry? Is it worth the expense?"

"It's a very decent computer. Do you need yours upgraded? If not, you'd probably be better off having all the files cleaned off and the settings returned to factory and then either donating the whole works or selling it for little or nothing. I wouldn't leave anything computer related here. The monitors and the security system are fine to leave. I imagine whoever buys this place will want a sophisticated security system. There's a lot of ground out there to cover. Will the guard dogs stay here?"

"I don't know about the dogs. I figured I would ask the new owners. If so, I'm willing to leave them and not charge anything for them. If not, I will have to cross that bridge later. They're smart, nice dogs. I just don't have a need for them."

Jerry sits down at the computer. "Let me do a little more checking. Then, I'll go get Milo and talk to my contacts at Interpol. Okay?"

"Sounds good. I'm going to contact a locksmith so I can get into this room before Sandra and her team comes tomorrow."

Chapter 33

Nothing is obvious and Jerry decides he wants more time later to snoop around on the computer, so he leaves to go pick up his dog and talk to his contacts at Interpol. I contact the locksmith company who says they can be here in about two or three hours and then I leave another message for Clark. "Clark, just thought I would fill you in on some developments here. Not sure if you're still having phone issues or if you're really busy. I have a locksmith coming for the door in the office but, other than that, nothing urgent. Call when you can. Can't wait to see you next week."

In about 10 minutes, the front gate signals someone is here. A man identifies himself as the locksmith and I let him in the gate. Within a couple of minutes he's ringing the doorbell. "Wow, that was fast. Thanks for being so prompt. You must live around here to get here so quickly." I welcome him inside.

"I was in the neighborhood." He's carrying a satchel type bag as he enters the foyer.

"Great. I'm sorry. I didn't get your name. I'm Marta, by the way."

"Tom. Where's the lock?"

Okay . . . man of few words. Let's get this done. "The door with the lock is in a room upstairs. I'll show you. I'm not sure but it seems like a complicated lock and I don't have the key. I inherited this place and the owner must have forgotten to give me the key. If you can't open it, I'm not sure what I'm going to do about it." It seems like as good an explanation as any as we head up the stairs.

Tom is following me kind of slowly and he appears to be looking around. He's probably impressed with the size and grandeur . . . just like most everyone. "This place is pretty impressive, Tom. Do you do a lot of work in this area? I don't believe your information told me where your office is located. Are you in the village?"

"Nope."

Okay. I'm not sure which question he answered. But, whatever. I just need him to get the door open; I don't need to have an in-depth conversation with him.

We enter the office suite and I motion to the door in the back corner. Tom looks around, sets his satchel down on the counter by the monitor, and pulls out a couple of tools.

"Does this look like it will be easy to open, Tom? Is there anything I can do?" I have more questions but Tom doesn't appear to be interested in answering any of them. He is standing in front of the door, blocking my view, silently working on the lock. I hear a whirring noise.

"You can wait downstairs if you want."

"No, that's okay. I'll get my purse and then wait here for you. What do I do when you get the door open? Can you make a key for me or is there a reason I need to keep this locked at all?"

No answer. Getting my purse from my bedroom, I come back in the office and see Tom still standing in front of the door. He turns around and points to the open door. "There."

"Wow, that was fast. Thanks, Tom. Will it lock again if shut it? Do I need a key?"

"Nope. I fixed it."

Assuming that means he fixed it so it won't lock, I smile and turn to him. "Thanks, again. What do I owe you?" I want to look inside the room, but I don't want to do that while Tom is here, so I wait impatiently while he hands me a handwritten bill. Once I pay him, I lead the way out of the office and down the stairs. I swear this man moves slower than a snail.

Finally, we're at the front door. Opening it, I again thank him. "Tom, I really appreciate you coming on such short notice and fixing that lock."

We walk outside where the dogs are sitting on the front steps. They don't bark at Tom or even sniff him. What's up with that? He looks around. "Are you selling the house soon?" This is the first complete sentence I think I've heard him utter and it's odd he would ask me about selling this place.

"As soon as I can, Tom. Why do you ask? Do you know someone who may be interested?"

"Nope." I guess he's back to one word answers. "Gotta go." With that he pats the dogs on the head and walks to his vehicle.

Several things strike me as odd when I watch him drive away; the dogs weren't alarmed by him one little bit, he's driving a very expensive car, his red ball cap covers his hair, and he's wearing thin gloves . . . ones like a nurse would wear. Did he have those on the whole time? Maybe he didn't want to get anything dirty in the office. I'm just not sure about this guy.

I wait for him to exit the gate and turn to the dogs. "I really wish you could talk. I'd like to know how you decide who to bark at. Who let you guys out of the back, anyway?" Stopping in my tracks, I look back toward the front gate. "Wait a minute. He reminds me of someone else. Who, though?"

As my phones buzzes, I see I have a message. "That's funny, I didn't hear it ring." It's the locksmith company telling me if I change my mind and need them again, they would be happy to send someone right over. "That's odd."

Chapter 34

Once back inside, I lock the front door behind me and head up-stairs to the office. My phone buzzes, telling me I've missed a call. I'm not sure how that happened as I had my phone with me the entire morning. I see it's from Clark, but he didn't leave a message. Strange. I'll call him back as soon as I look through the room in the office.

Entering the office suite, I see Shadow sitting on one of the desks. He's watching birds and ducks out on the grounds and meows as I enter. "Okay, Shadow, now I get to find out what's so important in this room that it had to be locked." I scratch his ears and head to the previously locked room.

It's dark in here and no automatic lighting comes on as I enter the room. I think to myself that this has to be the only room in the entire mansion without this feature. As I'm reaching for the light switch, the front gate signals someone is there. Going to the inter-com and monitor in the office, I see a man in a very nice car. "May I help you?"

"Yes. My name in Geoffrey and I'm from the Estate Place Auction House. I'm here for our appointment."

Oops. I had forgotten to check the day and time he was com-ing. "Geoffrey, I will open the gate. Please come to the front door."

Darn it. I really wanted to look in here, but I need to meet with Geoffrey, too. I guess the room will have to wait. The doorbell signals Geoffrey's arrival and I welcome him into the foyer. He's tall, well over six feet, and slim. Dressed impeccably in a dark grey suit, even his shoes are polished. I think to myself . . . he's exactly what a prominent auction house owner should look like.

Extending his hand to me, he is also the perfect gentleman. "As I said, my name is Geoffrey and I own the Estate Place Auction House as well as the Fine Arts Gallery in London. I believe we talked on the phone a couple of weeks ago. I also understand this is a difficult time for you and wasn't sure how much you remembered. Both of my businesses are pleased to have the opportunity to help you with the disbursement of your items. I would appreciate knowing if I am in competition for your business or not. I do believe you will find my estimates quite fair and understand that I will do everything I can to obtain the best results for you."

"Nice to meet you in person, Geoffrey. I'm Marta. First of all, thank you for taking time out of your schedule to come here. Your establishments were highly recommended by several people in the art and auction businesses. I have no desire to have anyone else take care of the items. You are the only one I want to work with.

"Having said that, I will look to you for guidance on how best to sell the items here. I have a spreadsheet with some questions for my art investigator and some questions for my agent listing this estate. That leaves some questions for you as well. I'm not sure how much you know about the history of this place. And, I'm not sure where or how you would like to start."

Geoffrey sets his briefcase down on a table in the foyer and removes his computer tablet. "Why don't we walk around and you can tell me what you don't want to keep? I will then either decide to place that item on one of my estate auctions or check to see if I have a client looking for such a piece. Would that work?"

"Certainly. But, I do need to tell you, I want to keep nothing from here. As I mentioned, my art investigator has a few items to check. They may have to be returned to their original owners. I'm not sure, yet. And, it's possible the buyers of this estate will want a few of the items."

"Fair enough. Are there some items on loan from collectors?"

Sighing, I decide I should tell him a little about the history here. "Geoffrey, I will fill you in on a brief history of the owner and this place. Maybe that will help you understand a little better." I give him a shortened version of Reid and finish with me inheriting all of it. I say nothing about him being my father. "So, you see we've been trying to get everything returned that didn't rightfully belong to him. Truthfully, it's a mess sorting it all out. That's why I have an art investigator and a jewelry expert involved."

Geoffrey has been nodding as I was talking. "I seem to remember something about some thefts but didn't connect those to the owner of this place. Everything must have been kept quiet, which isn't unusual. Okay, let's get started. I may be able to help you with some of your questions."

*C*hapter 35

Geoffrey is efficient and thorough as we work through the rooms downstairs. He asks questions and answers mine. We finish the upstairs bedrooms and I motion for us to enter the office suite. "I'm pretty sure the only things in here that will be suitable for auction are the two paintings on this wall and possibly these chairs. Otherwise, I'm leaving the security system for the new owners and have a computer person dismantling the rest."

"That's probably best. I'll add the chairs to the list. Oh, my." Geoffrey takes out his magnifying glass to inspect the first painting and then moves to the second one. "Have you had either of these authenticated?"

"No. This room was locked when my art investigator was here. He'll be back here next week and I'm hoping he can tell me about these two. Why?"

"Well, you have a couple of very nice Picasso paintings here."

"Oh dear. Do you suppose Reid actually paid for these or did he steal these as well? I'll have to ask Clark. How am I ever going to know for sure?"

"I can check to see if anyone has reported these two pieces missing. I'm sure your art investigator can do the same. We probably receive the same information about stolen art. If they don't show up on one of our bulletins, then my guess is he purchased them legitimately. You're sure you want to sell these? I know you have some valuable art and antiques downstairs, but these might be the most valuable in the whole place."

"Definitely, I want to sell everything. I want nothing from here."

Geoffrey smiles and nods in understanding. "That's fine with me. I just want to make sure as clients sometimes change their minds when they realize what they have. I realize you don't have that connection to the previous owner, and not everyone loves Picasso, anyway."

"Thanks for understanding. I already have so many wonderful things my grandma left to me. I honestly don't know where I'd put anything else. And, I certainly don't want a house as large as this one."

"Not everybody does. We're lucky some people do, though. It makes my job a whole lot more enjoyable. And, profitable. Is there anything else in this room? How about the doors? What do they lead to?"

"One is just a bathroom, although it's pretty large. Here take a look. There's nothing in here to sell, I believe." Opening the door, I motion for Geoffrey to enter.

"Not so fast, my dear. Take a look at this vase on the vanity and ohhh . . . look here. We have another Picasso. This man loved his Picassos, didn't he?"

"How about that. I can't believe it . . . in a bathroom. Why would you put a Picasso in a bathroom off the office?"

Chuckling at me, Geoffrey says, "Because you can."

Motioning to the other door, I tell him I haven't been in that room yet and explain about the locksmith leaving only moments before Geoffrey arrived. "In fact, you may have seen him on the road. He was driving a white, spiffy Mercedes AMG. He left shortly before you got here."

"Yes. Yes, I remember that car quite well. This positively wonderful, white Mercedes was driving down the very center of the road, coming straight at me. The driver had a phone in one hand

and motioning wildly with the other hand and it didn't appear he was paying any attention to driving. I tooted my horn several times before he pulled to his side of the road and sped off. I almost called the police but I didn't think quickly enough to get his license plate number. He was quite rude."

Chapter 36

"Well, I'm glad he opened this room for me. I doubt it has anything of interest in it. In fact, I was just going to look into it when you arrived." Finding the light switch, we see the room is quite large considering I figured it was a closet.

"Marta, it appears it's all equipment and gadgets. Two nice chairs, but I see nothing else of special interest to me. Let's go back downstairs and I can give you some things to think about and some pieces you may want to ask your listing agent about. Then we'll talk about dates. I have a nice auction coming up in a month. Some of these things would complement that sale quite nicely and I would still have time to get them listed in the catalogue. I've also been making a list of items where I want to contact collectors directly. You have some pieces here that would do better as a direct sale instead of being on an auction. Then, other items I would save for a larger sale I have in two months. Will this work for you?"

We've been walking down stairs as we talk. Shadow has come from a nap somewhere and is stretching as he follows us. "Oh my, what a gorgeous cat. Come here, love. You are just the sweetest thing." Geoffrey is enamored by Shadow and Shadow takes his praise as if it was due.

"He's my friend and right now my roommate in this huge place. He loves attention and once you pet him, you have a friend for life."

"I can see that, Marta. I love cats and even have a couple in my office. They're such good companions. Now, let's look at my notes."

We spend the next half hour going over his notes, making to do lists, and firming up dates. "Geoffrey, I'm going to be leaving here in the next couple of weeks. I'm due in Venice. Will that be a problem?"

"Not at all. You really don't need to be here for any of the sales. If I have any questions, you can leave a number where you can be reached. I'll handle everything for you. This will be exciting. I'm going to research the Picassos and please ask your art consultant to do so as well. I want to cover all bases on those pieces before I contact my client who I know will be interested in having them for his collection.

"This has been an amazing time for me. I love looking at your fine things. Be sure to ask your agent about these items and get back to me as soon as you can. They would make a great addition to both sales. Plus, I have a client who collects crystal made by the same artist as yours."

Geoffrey hands me a sheet to give to Sandra, a sheet for me, and puts his paperwork back in his briefcase.

"Geoffrey, thank you so much for coming. It's been interesting seeing all these things from your professional point of view. And, I will let you know what Sandra and Clark have to say."

As he heads out the front door, I expect to see the dogs sitting there. But, they are nowhere to be seen. I could have sworn I let them back into the front area, but apparently not.

"Bye, Marta. I'll be in touch. Thanks again for choosing my business."

Closing the door, I head to the kitchen to grab a light snack to take to the office with me. "Shadow, I want to look through the room before Jerry returns. Then, he can help me decide what to do about it."

Heading upstairs, I check my phone to see if I missed any calls. "I also need to call Clark. I'll call him while I'm in the office room and maybe he can tell me what I'm looking at in there. I didn't get much of a chance to see anything when Geoffrey and I were there. I could tell it was of no interest to him, Shadow."

Shadow doesn't seem interested in following me as I open the now unlocked door, flip on the light switch, and look around once more. One wall has several small machines with blinking lights. "These must be for the security system." There's a large screen on another wall. "Hmmm . . . I wonder what that is for. Where do I turn it on?" Two small file cabinets sit along a third wall with two comfy looking, soft, cream colored leather chairs in front of them. "This is like an office in an office. Weird. I'd like to figure out what this screen is hooked up to. There has to be a button to turn it on somewhere on it. I should have brought a flashlight so I could see behind it."

Bending over and feeling around to see if I can find a button, my back is to the door to this room. Just as I think I've reached something underneath that feels like a power button, the room goes dark and the door slams shut.

Chapter 37

"What the hell? What happened?" It's pitch black in here and I bump my head as I straighten up. I can't see a thing. I can't hear a thing. "Which way is the door? Let's see, I think it's over this way." Turning slowly, I move with my hands outstretched in front of me. I bump into what I remember as the leather chairs. "Okay, I'm going the right way. Wait. I have my cell phone. It has a light on it." Reaching in my pocket, I pull out my phone and press the on button. Nothing happens. "What's the deal? I know it's charged."

Fumbling in the dark with it, I try the button again. "That's the right button. But, nothing is working. Why would that be?"

Realizing my phone isn't going to help me, I go back to fumbling, moving slowly around the room. The blinking lights from the two machines give me a little light as my eyes are beginning to adjust to the darkness. "I can do this. It's a big room but not that big, for goodness sake."

Eventually, I feel what appears to be a flat wall. "Okay. This is good. This should be the wall where the door is located." Sure enough, I feel the door. Moving my hands down, I touch the doorknob. "Yay. I found it." Turning the knob, nothing happens. In fact, the knob doesn't even turn. "What? It can't be locked. Tom fixed it, right?"

I struggle with the knob and it still doesn't budge. Now, I'm getting nervous. No one knows where I am, Jerry isn't due back for at least an hour, and he probably won't think to look in here anyway. He still thinks this room is locked. In fact, I can't remember if he took the key to the front door.

"Okay. Think." Trying the knob one more time doesn't get me anywhere. Feeling for the hinges, I wonder if I can do anything with them. "Maybe I should beat on the door. What good would that do? Nobody is here." I pull out my phone again. It still doesn't work.

"Don't panic. I need to figure this out. Think. What all did I see in here before the lights went out? The lights. Wait. Where is the light switch? Why didn't I think of that earlier?" Feeling along the wall, my hand brushes the light switch and I flip it up. Light fills the room. "What is going on? I had the lights on, so how did they turn off? I didn't hear anyone, either. Is there someone here? Why wouldn't the dogs alert me?"

Now I look at my phone and see it still isn't working. It's like it's completely dead and I know for a fact it is fully charged. "Could it be this room?"

Moving to the large screen, I look again for some way to turn it on. "Aha. Here's a remote control. Maybe that works." Picking it up and looking at it, I mutter. "This has to be the oddest remote I've ever seen. No channels, no volume control, nothing that my remotes have. But, here's a power button. Let's try it."

Sure enough, when I point the remote at the large screen and hit the power button, the screen comes to life. I'm looking at a gigantic computer screen with a menu and folders. "Let's see if this remote has a way I can point to one of the folders or the menu." I try several buttons on the remote and nothing happens. Nothing opens on the screen. Nothing even indicates I'm pointing at anything. "That's odd."

Reading the menu, I see several choices listed; security, admin, tools, messages, personnel, and acquisitions. The folders don't have names, but there are several of them. Each one has a number. They don't open, either.

"Okay. This is getting me nowhere. At least not out of here. This is a puzzle for Jerry. What else is here? I wonder what these other machines are for. They almost look like DVD players. Why would you have DVD players in here? Or, maybe this was Reid's hideaway when he wanted to watch movies alone. That doesn't make sense. He has a whole stupid house, for goodness sake. Okay, let's look at the cabinets."

Starting with the cabinet closest to one of the comfy chairs, I pull the bottom drawer open. It's heavy and it sticks a little, but I manage it. And, I just about drop it. "Good thing my foot wasn't in the way. It would be crushed by now." Looking inside, I see the reason why it's so heavy. There's a dark green metal box, about 10 inches square and at least three inches tall. "Oh. Maybe this is where Reid kept his gold." Now, I'm being sarcastic.

Struggling with the box, I finally work my fingers underneath it and get it up to the side of the drawer. Taking a breath, I keep my hand braced on the box so I don't drop it back into the drawer. "Whoa. This is really heavy. What's it made of, anyway?" Taking a deep breath, I push the box onto the carpet and it lands on its side with a thud. "Okay, I've had my weight training for the day. Now, let's see if this thing opens."

Tipping the box so it's sitting right side up, I see a tumbler lock on it. "Damn. Of course it's locked. Why wouldn't it be? I really don't want to call the locksmith, Tom, back here. Maybe I can play with some numbers and see what happens."

*C*hapter 38

Trying countless, random combinations of numbers, gets me nothing and I'm frustrated. Out of habit, I glance at my phone to see what time it is. "Well, that's stupid, Marta. Your phone doesn't work. Remember?" Once again I'm talking to myself. This time I don't even have Shadow to talk to.

My frustration is turning to severe annoyance. "How long before someone finds me? There has to be something I can do. I'm going to try one more combination and then I'm going to start banging on the door. At least I'll feel like I'm doing something. Why, oh why, didn't I block open this door?" I'm annoyed at myself, at the stupid door, at Reid . . . you name it.

Looking at the combination tumbler's numbers again, this time I try to think like a thief. After all, I'm positive this had to belong to Reid. "What would he think is an important number and one he can remember? What would make sense to him? Maybe it's this address." Turning to those numbers, nothing happens. "Is it art related or something less obvious? Is it Picasso's birth date? He seemed to like him. How would I know Picasso's birth date, anyway?" I try another set of random numbers. Again, nothing is working.

"Damn. Maybe it's my birthday. Ha. That would really make me mad." Thinking I have nothing to lose by trying my birth date, I enter the combination of six numbers. And hear a soft click.

"Well, double damn." I don't know whether to be furious or scared. "Why would he use my birthday? I didn't think he knew my birthday and I certainly don't ever remember him giving me a birthday gift when I was little. This is too bizarre." I sit back in the chair and stare at the box. "No time like the present to see what he kept in here."

Opening the cumbersome lid with my fingertips, I see why the box is so heavy. It's about 10 inches square, but the walls or sides must be an inch thick and the lid is about two inches thick. "This is one well-constructed box. And, it looks old." The first thing I see when I lift the lid is a purple velvet cloth with some initials or possibly a monogram. "Pretty. Wonder what is under it, though."

Lifting the soft, rich cloth and setting it aside, I'm not sure what I was expecting to see. But, I do know it wasn't this. "Oh my." I desperately wish my phone was working. I'd like to take a picture and send it to Clark and Sam. Glancing at my phone, I see the text message symbol is lit up. "What? I didn't hear a text come in. Is it working now?" Trying to retrieve the message, I get nothing.

Laying my phone down, I go back to the treasure in the box and sit and stare at it, almost afraid to touch it. Almost. "I wonder who it really belongs to. Maybe the initials on the cloth are a clue."

Glimmering up at me is the most stunning necklace I have ever seen. Dainty, filigree gold floats around diamonds and emeralds, displaying a perfect circle. More substantial gold holds the circle together. Picking it up, it's not as heavy as I first thought it might be. As the diamonds and emeralds catch the light, they absolutely shimmer, casting tiny, dancing prisms all over the room. "Oh my goodness. This is breathtaking. Why on earth would Reid have this? Wait. He probably stole it from someone. But, who? Who would have something like this? And, why lock it up. Did he ever take it out and look at it?"

As I start to return the necklace to the box, I notice a small picture that was lying beneath the necklace. "Aha. Maybe this will tell me who the necklace belongs to." Carefully setting the necklace on the velvet cloth, I pick up the picture . . . only to see it's not really a picture, in the sense I first thought. It's a small oil painting. Looking closely at it, the detail is amazing for this three inch by three inch piece of art.

There's a lady, dressed in a formal gown, sitting on a chair. But, the focus of the painting is most definitely on what she is wearing. This necklace. "Okay. Now I have a face to go with the owner. But, who is this? She looks a little like other paintings I've seen. I just don't know where. And, I know I've never seen this necklace before.

"I really need to talk to Clark. In fact, I really need to get out of here. How long have I been here? My snack is gone and I'm hungry, so it's probably been at least an hour. Why can't I figure out how to get out? Why doesn't my stupid phone work? What if no one finds me? What if I die in here? "

My annoyance is quickly turning to panic with all the questions running through my head.

Looking up at the Heavens, "Grandma, did you know about this necklace?" Leaning back in the chair, I touch my gold coin. The previously locked door to the office opens. Shadow comes running in as Jerry says "What is going on? What are you doing in here? Are you okay?"

Chapter 39

"Shadow, Jerry . . . am I glad to see both of you." Picking up a purring Shadow, he rubs his head on my chin. "Jerry, how did you find me? How did you get into the house?"

"Marta, we need to sit down and talk. I'll explain what's been going on."

"What do you mean, what's been going on? What time is it?" Moving to the door to prop it open, "Jerry, don't let this door shut."

Jerry picks up a book, puts it in front of the door, and motions for me to sit back down. That's when he notices the heavy box and the necklace. "Whoa, what on earth is that? Where did you get it?"

"It's a long story. You go first. What's been going on?"

"Okay. But, you need to listen to the whole story. Deal?"

I nod my head and sit down as Shadow curls up on my lap. "Deal."

"Let me start from when I left this morning. I hadn't gone very far when I noticed a car behind me. This was the same car sitting just outside your front gate. I took some turns and a couple of detours and the car kept following me, sometimes far back and once in a while closer to me. I couldn't see the driver as the windows were quite dark. I pulled onto a side street and let him pass by so I could get his license plate. Only, there wasn't one.

"So, I called the local police and filled them in. They're still looking for the car. Once I let him go by, I went on home, made a bunch of phone calls, got the mail, and picked up Milo. Then, we ran some errands and we headed here."

"Okay. So far, so good. Where is Milo?"

"He's outside with the shepherds. They're doing fine together. But, now here's where things aren't so fine. Milo and I arrived at the front gate and I used the code. I didn't have a key to the house but figured you would be home, anyway. I took Milo around back, introduced him to the dogs, and they all took off running like they were long lost friends. When I took my things out of the truck and started up the front steps is when I noticed things weren't quite right."

"What do you mean?"

"For starters, the front door was slightly ajar. So, I grabbed my weapon and slowly pushed open the door. I heard nothing. Coming in a little further, I still heard nothing. That's when I called your name. Nothing. No one in the kitchen, no one in the rest of the rooms downstairs, or anywhere. Shadow didn't even come to see what was going on, even though I called his name."

"The front door was open? I distinctly remember closing and locking it after Geoffrey left."

"Geoffrey? Who is that?"

"He is the owner of Estate Place Auction House in London. He came right after Tom, the locksmith was here."

"I've heard of that auction place and believe they have a great reputation."

"That's what Clark told me, Jerry. That's why I contacted them to disperse of the things here. But, back to the front door. It was locked before I came up here. I was just going to look around a little until you got here. But, the minute I walked in and started to look around, the lights went out, the door slammed shut, and I couldn't get it open." I pause as Jerry nods.

"Okay. Let me continue and we can piece together the rest. When I couldn't find you downstairs, I came upstairs to look around. First, I went to the bedroom where I'm staying and found

125

nothing out of the ordinary. The rest of the bedrooms had nothing in them either. Until, that is, I went into yours."

"Why? What did you find?"

"Since I know you aren't a slob, I was a little surprised by the condition of your bedroom when I first looked in. Then, I stepped into the room, calling your name. Marta, your room is trashed. Things are strewn all over, some things in your bathroom are broken, drawers are open, and your closet is a mess. It really looked like someone couldn't find what they were looking for, so they just got mad and threw everything on the floor. In a few minutes I'll take you there to see if anything is missing."

My mouth is hanging open and I start to get up. Jerry puts his hand on my arm. "Marta, in a couple of minutes we'll go there and look. Right now, Interpol is in there looking for fingerprints and clues. They'll come here when they are finished."

"Interpol?" I manage to squeak out. "What? Why?"

"There's more, Marta. And, that's why I called Interpol. I also left Clark a message."

Chapter 40

"More? What do you mean by more?"

Taking a deep breath, Jerry looks me in the eyes. "This is why I called Interpol and Clark. This is personal. It's not just a random break-in. Written on the mirror in your bathroom are the words 'give it up now bitch.' Whoever wrote it used a pink lipstick, probably yours. It's all in caps, covering most of one mirror, and I'd guess by the heavy look to the print the person who wrote this was angry."

My lips are pursed, my hands clenched in my lap, and I don't seem to be breathing. Holding Shadow tighter, "What does that mean? Why me? What do I have? Is all this still connected to Reid? Is this connected to me being here? Do you think someone locked me in here?" I have dozens more questions, but Jerry touches my hand and I look directly at him.

"Marta, we all have questions. And, we're going to get to the bottom of this. I have more to tell you that will hopefully make you feel a little better. Then, you're going to tell me why you're here and what's going on in this room. Okay?"

"Okay."

"After I realized you weren't in your bedroom and nowhere to be found, I started looking for Shadow. I couldn't find him, either.

I looked in all the spots I figured a cat would hide. Nothing. You're going to have to show me his special hiding places.

"Then, Interpol arrived and we searched the house some more. No sign of you or of Shadow. They went to work in your bedroom and are also dusting for prints on the front door. That's when I had a . . . I'm not sure what to call it. It wasn't a vision. More of a strong feeling." Jerry, the by-the-book Marine and Interpol agent who deals with facts, is trying to describe what happened. I smile at the struggle going on in his mind.

"Jerry, please keep going. I think I get it. It just felt like you knew what to do next. Right?"

"Right. It seems weird, though. Anyway, I had this sensation that you were in the office and in trouble. I had been in here a couple of times looking for you and didn't see you. But, this time when I walked in, Shadow was sitting right outside this door." Jerry points to the door to the room I was locked in. "When I approached him, he started meowing and scratching on the door. It was the darnedest thing. He kept looking back at me and meowing, like he was telling me where you were. I figured the door was still locked, but when I tried the handle, it opened right up." Jerry gets up to turn the knob from the inside and it doesn't budge.

"That's really odd. It works from the outside, but not from the inside. Who would ever design something like that?" Sitting back down and looking at me, "Now, you tell me what happened?"

"Okay." I tell him about Tom, the locksmith, being here. I leave out nothing, including what I notice about him after he left, how quickly he got here, and then Geoffrey's impression of Tom driving away from here. Jerry is taking notes as I'm talking.

Then, I move on to Geoffrey coming and our tour of the house. Finally, I give him the events that happened once I entered this room, including finding this box. I motion to the box as he looks at it.

Moving Shadow off my lap, I bend down and pick up the purple cloth and necklace lying beside it. Then, I lift the lid off the box and retrieve the painting I had dropped when I heard the door open. I watch as Jerry carefully holds the necklace up to the light and then looks at the small painting.

"Wow." He looks at me.

"I know. I assume it's stolen, like most of Reid's acquisitions and treasures. I'll have to call Sam about this one. Isn't it just the most fantastic piece you've ever seen? And, how about this little painting? Look at the detail. The thing is, the woman reminds me of someone. I just have no idea who. Clark will need to look at this. Speaking of Clark, I need to call him. You said you talked to him? What did he say?"

"First, I did call Clark. But, the call went right to his voice mail. He must be really busy. I haven't talked to him in days. That's why I called Interpol.

"Second, this is quite the find. I do wonder why it's hidden here, unless it was a recent theft and he didn't want to take the chance anyone would see it displayed downstairs. It's obvious the painting and the necklace go together, though. Look at the woman in the painting. She is wearing this necklace."

"I know. And, to my untrained art eye . . . the setting in the painting seems old. It just doesn't look like it's a recent scene. But, I guess it could be made to look that way. I was just starting to look at all the machines in here, but figured I probably wouldn't know exactly what they did. I do want you to look at them when we're done with Interpol. Speaking of Interpol, should we go see what they've found?"

Chapter 41

"Good idea, Marta. They are probably about finished anyway. First, though, let's figure out a way to make it so this door doesn't shut and lock again on either one of us."

"That's definitely fine by me. I never want to feel locked in here again, even though I found this fabulous necklace. I need to take a photo with my cell phone and send it to Sam. Maybe he has a clue if this has been stolen in the last year or so. Wait. I forgot to tell you. My cell phone wouldn't work in here, even though it indicated I received a text message. Look." I touch the on button . . . and it works just fine. "That's odd. It wouldn't turn on at all, and I tried several times."

"Please let me see it, Marta." I hand it to Jerry and he walks around the room with it. It works in all parts of this room. "I'm not sure what to make of that. It's working fine now. I'll fiddle with it when we're finished talking to Interpol." He hands the phone back to me and I check the text message. Nothing. "I know it signaled a message coming in. What's going on with it?"

"No idea." Jerry props open the door as I put the purple cloth, necklace, and painting back in the metal box. "Let's leave everything here, visit with Interpol, and then come back to inspect this room. Okay?"

"Fine with me." Just as we enter into the office suite from the previously locked room, two agents from Interpol are coming in to see us. Jerry introduces us all.

"Marta, agents Peter Collins and Thomas Green from the Interpol office in London. Peter and Thomas, this is Marta. What have you found?"

Both nod as we shake hands and exchange formalities. Peter looks at Jerry and then at me. "We've dusted for prints in several places but found none. In fact, we noticed your room was absolutely clean of any fingerprints, Marta. Do you know if you wiped down everything in there today?"

Chuckling, "I'm sure I've not wiped anything down since I arrived about a week ago. My prints should be all over everything. Along with Shadow's paw prints."

"Well, there are no prints on your dresser, your jewelry box, nightstand, the toilet stool handle, the mirror, and even none on your hairbrush. It's obviously been cleaned by whoever was in there. We do want to show you the mirror, even though it's quite disturbing considering what you went through last year. Are you ready to see it?"

"Yes, I am. Lead the way." We all head down the hall to my bedroom and Thomas stops me before we enter through the closed door. "Marta, we are finished in here and we had to move some of your things. We can help you pick up the rest if you like."

I nod as we enter my bedroom. Clothes are thrown all over the floor and bed, sheets are no longer on the bed, contents of my dresser drawers are on the floor, my suitcases are open and in the middle of the room, my jewelry box is smashed, and my shoes are everywhere. In the bathroom, my make-up is strewn all over the counter and floor. Some things are destroyed, others just flung about. Written in pink lipstick on the counter- to-ceiling mirror above the sinks are the words Jerry told me about. Big, bold words.

GIVE IT UP NOW BITCH

"Yes, that's my lipstick, or at least it was. What does it mean? Jerry, do you think it has to do with what I found in the locked room?"

Jerry looks at me. "It definitely could be. It seems worthy enough to want.I certainly think anyone would like to have that."

At the quizzical looks from the agents, Jerry says, "Marta was locked in a room for quite a while this afternoon and found an amazing piece of jewelry. Come back to the office and we'll show you. It could be what this is all about. You also need to hear what she has to tell you about the locksmith. I think he has something to do with this."

Chapter 42

We all head back to the office, enter what I'm now thinking of as the interior room, and I show the necklace to the agents. "Do you suppose this is what that message on my mirror refers to?"

They both nod and Peter is the first to speak. "I would bet money on it. This looks like a spectacular piece. What thief wouldn't want it?"

Thomas takes the purple, velvet cloth and is looking at the initials. "Do these mean anything to you, Marta? They really look like family initials or a monogram, the way they're written. And, this isn't just an ordinary piece of material. It has some weight to it. Almost like it was meant to be paired with the necklace. Look at that painting. You need to have Clark look closely at it. He might be able to tell you more about the lady or the timeframe when it was painted. Do you have a safe place to keep these? I know this room was locked, but is there a safe here?"

At the mention of Clark's name, I react. "I didn't know you knew Clark. In fact, I was going to call him again. I keep getting his voice mail. As for a safe, good question. I haven't come across one and that's odd, don't you think? I mean with all this security and antiques . . . why wouldn't there be a safe?"

Thomas nods. "First, good question about the safe. There has to be one. Jerry, why don't you look for one? Second . . . yes, we know Clark. Jerry here introduced us several years ago and he's done some work for us on different cases. He's a good resource. I do know he's busy in Dubai but I'll try to call him, too."

As I'm putting the necklace back in the box, Jerry is in the outer office looking at the different monitors and calls to the agents. "Hey guys, come here. The security camera that looks directly at the front door has been disabled. Look. Nothing but black on this one. I'm positive it was working yesterday."

Coming out of the interior room, I join the conversation. "It most definitely was working. In fact, it worked today when Geoffrey from the auction house was here. I used it to see who was here this morning. What's wrong with it?"

"It appears this monitor, and maybe more, have been disabled. I'll work to see if I can reconstruct what was here. I'm sure it has memory in it."

"Jerry, you do your thing with it and we'll get going to work from our end. We need to double check all of our findings here, put out some bulletins, talk to local police to see if they picked up anything off their security, and check our files on stolen jewelry to see if your necklace appears anywhere, Marta. Keep it safe. In fact, do check for a safe on the premises. Keep in mind, the thief didn't find what he was looking for. He may be back. You both need to be careful. Okay?"

"Thanks. I think I'll take a photo of the necklace and email it to Sam in Venice. He or his resources may also be able to tell us more about it. And, I'm going to figure out what the initials on the cloth are. Will you get in touch with Jerry and me to let us know what you find?"

"Yes. We'll do our work and stop back here tomorrow."

"I do have the real estate agent and her team coming tomorrow, but I'm not sure what time. I'll find out. I don't think it's a good idea for them to be here when you are, do you?"

"No, I agree. Right Thomas? Marta, can you think of anyone who wants what you have? With the phone calls you've been getting and now this break-in, someone thinks you have something valuable. It definitely could be the necklace. But, that means he or she knew about it from Reid. And, that means Reid either had assistants we don't know about, bragged too much about it to the wrong people, or something else entirely."

At the mention of assistants, I remember what Priscilla told me. "Agents, there may be an assistant."

"What do you mean, may be?"

"When I was getting the keys from Priscilla, I asked her for the key to this room and the computer passwords. She told me I would have to get them from Reid's assistant. I had no idea what she was talking about and she didn't answer when I asked her. Do you suppose he really did have an assistant who is trying to get his hands on this necklace?"

"That's a definite possibility. We'll do some checking of his known associates. A name or face might ring a bell."

My phone indicates I have a text from Sandra. Reading it, I relay the message to the agents. "Sandra and her team will be here tomorrow at 10 o'clock. I'm thinking they only have about an hour or two of work left to do and will be gone by noon. If you need to come back, anytime in the afternoon would work."

"Thanks, Marta. Jerry, see you tomorrow. Let us know what you find on that monitor and security camera."

Chapter 43

Jerry is working on the monitor and security camera, the agents have left, Shadow is sleeping in the office window, and I head to my bedroom to clean up the mess. "No sense having it looking like this for Sandra."

An hour later I've cleaned the entire bedroom suite, made a pile of broken items to throw away, started laundry, decided I need to purchase two new suitcases, and found my jewelry that somehow made its way under the bed. "I'm really glad I found these pieces." Even though the bracelets are gold, they're not priceless pieces. "I'm also glad I'm wearing my coin necklace and one of the rings I kept from Grandma's collection."

Touching my coin, I have a feeling I need to call Clark. Right now. "What's up with this necklace? I swear it tells me what to do." Sitting down on one of the now clean chairs in my bedroom, I place a call to Clark. Once again, it goes right to voicemail. "Hey, Clark. I know you're really busy. I need to fill you in on a bunch of things here, though. I had a break-in, my bedroom was trashed, I was locked in a room, and two agents from Interpol were here. They know you. Agents Peter Collins and Thomas Green. I found another necklace. Jerry is trying to fix the front door camera, I let Priscilla go, and let's see . . . what else has been going on? It seems like a lot. Call me when you can and let me know when you'll be here. Bye."

Hanging up, I try to remember the last time I had an actual conversation with Clark. I think it was at least a couple of days ago, before Jerry got here.

Thinking of Jerry, I decide to see how he's doing and head back to the office. "Hey, Marta. I just about have the camera working again. I'm pretty sure it didn't just fail all by itself as several connections were unplugged. Since I'm sure they didn't just fall out all at the same time, someone had to unplug them. You're sure you looked at this monitor, the one that showed the front door, when the auction guy was here?"

"Positive. I had let Tom, the locksmith, out and I came up here as I wanted to inspect this inner room. About the time I figured out where the light switch was, the front gate signaled someone was there. I came out of that room to check the monitor . . . oh wait a minute. I didn't use it to check the front door, only to see who was at the front gate. Once I saw who it was, I went downstairs to let Geoffrey in. I didn't use that one to look at the front door. So, it could have been disabled for some time.

"I remember Sandra and I looked at the monitors and cameras out back the first day she was here and I'm almost sure I looked at the front door monitor when you arrived. Yes, I know I did. You reminded me of Clark when I saw you standing on the front step."

"So, Marta, it could have been disabled by your locksmith. He was the only one around this monitor. Right?"

"Yes, he was and I suppose he could have done that. Except, wouldn't it take a while? He did tell me I could wait downstairs, but I didn't. I stayed right here, once I got my purse out of my bedroom, and he seemed to work quickly. I was only out of this room for a few of minutes. Let me think. I heard some whirring and he had his tool case with him, but I didn't really pay close attention to him. He had his back to me the whole time, purposely blocking my view of the door and this area. Could he have done this in a short amount of time?"

"Probably. Especially if he knew what he was doing. How did you happen to pick him as the locksmith?"

"I didn't really pick him specifically. I called the first company listed in the area when I checked the Internet. And, now that you mention it, they told me someone would be here in a couple of hours. But, Tom came almost immediately. Then, right after he left, I had a voice mail from the company thanking me for checking with them and telling me they would send someone here next time I needed them. It was odd."

"The message wasn't from Tom?"

"No."

"Did he give you an invoice?"

"Not really. Just a handwritten piece of paper that gave the amount I owed and I paid him in cash. It's funny. I used US dollars out of habit and he didn't say anything. I guess I was in such a hurry to get this room open, it didn't dawn on me at the time."

Chapter 44

"Marta, do you remember the name of the locksmith company?"

"Yes. It's right here." I pick up another piece of paper with their number on it, hand it to Jerry, and he makes a call. After a couple of minutes, he nods, tells them thank you, and turns to me. "We have a problem. They don't have an employee by the name of Tom. And, they have a message from you telling them to cancel the appointment."

"What? I didn't call them to cancel. The only call I made was to schedule."

"I know, Marta. It seems it was a male voice who called them and told them the lock was fixed."

"Oh no, Jerry. Do you think it was Tom? Do you think he disabled something on the camera and monitor? Why would he do that?"

"We can only assume at this point. If I can get this working we might have a better clue. You did say he was wearing gloves, right?"

"Right. And, his cap hid his face, for the most part. He really didn't want to be noticed."

"Or, remembered. Can you describe him at all?"

"That's true. He didn't really have any distinguishable or memorable features either. Let's see, he was wearing a red ball cap without a logo on it, his hair didn't stick out of it so I'm not exactly sure what color it was, he was about six feet tall, broad shoulders and an athletic build . . . not skinny but not overly muscular. He didn't really smile and he only talked in short, one word sentences. He did ask me when I was selling this place, I believe. That was the only time I heard him actually speak an entire sentence. He didn't really want to carry on a conversation with me, it seemed. Oh, and he wasn't British. At least he didn't sound British."

"Okay, that's good. What was he wearing and what was he driving?"

"He was wearing blue jeans, a gray t-shirt, black shoes, and the red cap. Nothing you would notice if you saw him anywhere. His car, however, was noticeable. It was a newer, white Mercedes AMG, very clean and shiny. In fact, Geoffrey mentioned it when he arrived."

"What do you mean, Marta?"

"Geoffrey said a really nice looking white Mercedes was driving pretty fast down the middle of the road towards him, a couple of miles from here. When he honked at him, he moved to the side of the road so Geoffrey wouldn't hit him, and then sped up. He thought the driver was wearing a red cap of some kind, so we figured it must be Tom. The odd thing now that I think about it, Tom left at least 10 or 15 minutes before Geoffrey showed up. Why was he just a couple of miles from here in that amount of time?

"What do you make of that, Jerry?"

"I'm not sure but I'm going to give all that information to Agents Peter and Thomas. It does seem rather strange with him showing up so quickly and the company having no idea about him. Something isn't quite right, but I can't put my finger on it."

"If it's okay with you, Jerry, I'm going to get us a glass of wine and make dinner. It's been too long since I've eaten and my mind is exhausted."

"Excellent idea, my dear. I'm just about finished with this system and maybe we can see something. I'll meet you in the kitchen in a few minutes."

Shadow joins me and eats while I fix dinner and Jerry is working in the office. "Shadow, there has to be something wrong with this whole estate. How many more treasures will I find here? And, who wants them enough to threaten me? Don't they realize I didn't even know Reid? And, why hasn't Clark returned my calls? I think I'll try him again right now."

Once more, the call goes right to his voice mail. "Damn, this is getting ridiculous. Okay, here's one more message.

"Clark, it's me again. Just really wanting to touch base. Please call me as soon as you can. Jerry and I have lots of news to tell you and he's going to have Interpol investigate the locksmith. Bye."

Jerry comes into the kitchen and picks up Shadow. "Well, I have the monitor and the camera working again and I reconstructed the last few days of the camera footage. I would bet money, given the time frame, that Tom was the one who disabled everything. It isn't hard, really. You just need to know what order to unplug everything, then move the cords, and turn all the switches off. It's sophisticated but not complicated, if you know what you're doing."

"So, did you find anything?"

"The last footage reveals a man with a cap covering his face. That has to be Tom. The one prior to that is a man and a lady. From your descriptions and the photos, I assume they are Special Agent Mark and Priscilla."

"Really? That was two days ago. Wait, a minute. Did they arrive together?"

"Almost but not in the same car. Priscilla arrives a couple of seconds before Mark, in a dark gray car, and has a driver who lets her out of the back seat. That strikes me as odd, for a housekeeper. The driver then gets back in the car and apparently stays there. I don't see him getting out again until right before Priscilla comes out of the house. He opens the door again for her and they drive off.

"Mark arrives, like I said, almost immediately after Priscilla. He's driving a black Mercedes and they appear to chat as they walk up to the front door. He leaves some time after her. When I look closely at the front door camera, it appears like he is in a hurry to leave. The front gate camera shows the same thing; he's in a hurry. Those are the last images from that camera.

"After I looked at the lock, I do have a couple of concerns. It is really a sophisticated lock, and probably a custom one. I can't help but wonder why. Another thing, Tom must be quite skilled at these special types of locks in order to get it open quickly. That bugs me."

Chapter 45

"Knowing that, it bugs me, too. He opened it rather quickly, even though he told me I could wait downstairs. That doesn't really make sense. It also bothers me that he wasn't from the locksmith company I called. How would he know I needed one? Do you suppose Mark or Priscilla told him? I may have mentioned getting a locksmith to both of them."

"I've thought of that. The timing is a little off, but it could be. Things are just not adding up."

We finish dinner and head back into the office to look more at the interior room. Jerry looks at the machines, monitors, and equipment while I start on the file cabinets. Looking through the cabinets I see dozens of files on people and antiques. Many of the stolen antiques have already been returned to their original owners and I lay those files aside. Perhaps Interpol or Clark will want those. I start looking at ones I don't recognize.

After almost two hours, Jerry is muttering to himself and comes to see what I've been doing. "What do you have there, Marta?"

I explain my piles to him and ask what he found. "Well, several things. It appears Reid kept digital files, photos, and information on pieces he was looking to acquire. That group of files gives info on where a particular piece is located, it lists detailed security about that place, and I do mean detailed security, and plans on how to acquire it. It's funny. He never uses the word steal or anything. He always says acquire.

"Then, he has one file on people and places. As near as I can figure out, I think there are two separate ways he was looking at people; one has to do with the person, collector, or place that owns the item and one has to do with who is going to be eliminated. He doesn't actually say murder, just eliminate. And, he doesn't say why. No idea if he didn't like the person or if he had other reasons to get rid of them. It's weird. Another thing, he also goes into great detail about the home or museum in this file as well.

"It appears nothing was left to chance. Now, here's another odd part that goes with what Priscilla told you. In several places he mentions his assistant will take care of that. He has lists of work, to do lists, contact lists . . . all for his assistant."

"Wow. Some of that fits exactly with the paper files I've found. Why do you suppose he would keep a paper file and also an online file? Maybe he was more OCD than we thought. Does this assistant have a name?"

"Yes, I believe he's referencing his assistant in several places. He calls him Gino. Does that name ring any bells?"

"No, not at all. Never heard of a Gino and Priscilla never mentioned anyone by the name of Gino."

"Marta, there are two more disturbing files, each on one person."

"Okay. Who?"

"One file is solely correspondence from one particular person. It's quite obvious this person is in law enforcement, but Reid doesn't say where he's from or what agency. However, this person does have intimate knowledge of all the murders, thefts, agencies involved, investigations, and more. He keeps Reid informed of everything that's going on and, in fact, allows Reid to stay one step ahead of any investigation. It's quite the sophisticated system they had worked out and it's lengthy and detailed. Interpol is going to want this one. There's never any mention of a name, however."

"While we were all in Italy there was an agent who was killed. I seem to remember Clark telling me that he was a dirty cop, but I don't think we knew his name."

"I'll have Interpol check."

"You said there were two files. Who is the second one about?" I'm dreading the answer as I have this feeling it isn't going to be good.

"Marta, the second file is also detailed and lengthy. It's all about you and your grandma."

$\mathcal{C}$hapter 46

I take a sharp breath. "Okay. What about us?"

"It starts from the time you moved to San Francisco. It seems he was most interested in the times when your grandma came to visit."

"What do you mean, Jerry?"

"Well, there are files on people the two of you met with and places you visited. These are detailed files, including times, descriptions, contact info, and photos. It's odd. It was like you were being tracked. But, nothing indicates why. He has some files that reflect just you, but those were immediately after your grandma left and went back to Minnesota. It seems he followed you for a day or two and then nothing until her next visit. What do you make of that, Marta? Any ideas?"

"Not at all. But, it appears he might have been more interested in the two of us together. Is that what you're seeing?"

"Yeah. I'm beginning to think that. He certainly has nothing on your grandma at her home or when she was alone and not much on you by yourself, unless it was just after she visited. I honestly don't know what he was doing, but I do know Interpol is going to want to see these files. I think, if it's okay with you, I'll make a trip to the London office tomorrow. I'll leave early, you can deal with the listing agent and her team, and I'll be back late afternoon. Okay?"

"That's fine. I think I'll turn in, then get up early with you, and try to get as much finalized as I can. This place is beginning to wear on me."

"Sounds like a plan. Good night, Marta."

Shadow and I head down the hall to bed and I sleep well considering all the thoughts running through my mind. Morning comes, Jerry and I eat breakfast, and he leaves for London with a vehicle full of computers, machines, files, paperwork, photos, and who knows what else. As far as I'm concerned, they can have everything if they'll just figure out what's going on . . . past and present.

"Shadow, we need to get more of this office cleaned out. Sandra and her team will be here soon. I think I have the rest of the place in order and just have some more to finish in the office and its interior room." Shadow follows me to the office as I start organizing and making lists as the front gate signals an arrival. At the same time, I receive a text from Sandra telling me they are here.

Welcoming them in, she introduces me to Ted, Lou's replacement. He's not nearly as friendly as Lou, doesn't make a lot of small talk, and gets right to business as Sandra and I chat. "Sandra, I am so sorry about Lou. Have the police found out anything more?"

"Not really. They're treating it as a probable robbery. He lived in a nice neighborhood and was home earlier than normal. If someone had been casing his place and thinking about breaking in, they wouldn't have expected him for at least another hour."

"Were things stolen?"

"I guess so. The police weren't real specific and his wife is pretty distraught. I haven't talked to her much about it."

"That's understandable. Okay. Where do you need to finish and what can I do to help? Oh, Geoffrey, from the Estate Place Auction House, was here. He went through everything and I have a list from him that I need to ask you about. He wants whatever your client doesn't. He'll take those items now or later . . . he doesn't care."

"That's great. Part of what we are doing today is making a list of items that make sense to offer to the buyer. We've already had two viable buyers contact us and both are in a hurry to see this estate. I want to get everything finalized here today, if that's okay with you."

"Perfect, Sandra. I will help with whatever you need."

Sandra and I spend the morning working off lists, Peter and Ted are off doing their things, and we all meet in the kitchen about one o'clock to have a light lunch. "Well, Marta, we're finished. We have a substantial list of items to offer to the buyers. They will need to make a decision about those items when they put in their offer. That way, Geoffrey will know exactly what he has for his clients or for auction. Will that be okay?"

"That's fantastic. What's the next step and what do you need me to do?

"Marta, we'll go back to the office now and contact the two interested parties. I'm sure they will want to see this estate as soon as possible. Both understand you are in the process of moving and selling some things, so don't worry about how everything looks."

"Do you want me to leave when you show it?"

"Not necessarily. You can be here; just not following us around. This is a big space and you can easily stay out of the way. That way, if there are some specific questions about how something works you can be available to answer them. Okay?"

"Sounds good to me." We finish lunch, they pick up their files, lists, equipment, and computers, and head out the door. I still haven't said more than a handful of words to Ted. But, he appears to do excellent work when I look at the detail on his spreadsheets.

After closing the front door behind them, it dawns on me I haven't seen Shadow all morning. "Shadow, where are you? Are you napping or hiding?" I pick up our lunch remnants in the kitchen and head upstairs to the office, looking for Shadow. He slinks out from behind a chair in the office, ears back, tail down, looking around. "What the heck got into you? I thought you liked Sandra and the guys."

He rubs up against my leg, purring. "Something must have spooked you. What was it? I really wish you could talk."

Chapter 47

Talking to myself again as Shadow has now apparently gone downstairs to eat, I survey the office one more time. "I'm pretty sure I'm finished in here. The security system has been cleaned up, Jerry has everything working, and it's all pretty straightforward. If the buyers don't want it, they can have it removed." I notice Jerry also took the computers with Reid's files out of the office, as well as those from inside the inner room. "I want to get this inner office completely cleaned out so the buyers can use this room as storage or for whatever."

Entering the inner office room, I prop open the door, sit down, and start to work on the few remaining paper files in case we need to keep any of them. I mutter to myself. "This room is looking much better. I will finish these and then we can move these cabinets out of here. We still haven't found a safe, so I really doubt there's one here. Kind of odd, but oh well. And, I almost forgot, I need to call Clark. I think I'll do that now."

Standing up, I look at my phone. It seems to work. "That is so strange that it wouldn't work when I was in here before. I don't get it." I get Clark's voicemail immediately. "Clark, I know you're really busy and I hate to keep bothering you, but I need to fill you in on a bunch of things. Jerry discovered all sorts of new information on some computer files here. You were right when you had him come here. He's at Interpol in London right now with everything. He found out Reid did indeed have an assistant, named Gino, we think. He also found information leading him to believe Reid had an inside contact, someone in law enforcement. He has a bunch more information about that as well.

"Geoffrey, from the auction house, has everything categorized and only has a couple of things to check on for authenticity. He was excited about the rest. Sandra and her team finished and have two clients they want to show this place to in the next couple of days. I'd better go. I'm sure your voicemail is full by now. Call when you can."

I've been walking around the inner office while talking and now that I'm finished with my message, I sit back down to empty the remaining two drawers and make piles of paper to destroy. "I'm almost done. Thank goodness these don't have much in them; just a few envelopes. Clark will be impressed with everything Jerry and I have done. Maybe he will get to meet Geoffrey and Sandra and her team. Her team . . . wait a minute. Ted . . . I'm positive I've seen him before. Where, though? Think, Marta, think."

Putting my head in my hands and shutting my eyes, I try to focus on his face. My necklace with the coin on it swings forward and I move it back inside my sweater.

The door to the inner office slams shut, I jump, and scream. "What the hell? Who's there?" I rush to the door but it won't open; the knob won't turn and the door won't budge at all. "I thought this knob was fixed so it wouldn't lock. What happened?" I shove at it some more and the result is the same. Nothing.

"At least I have lights. But, no one knows I'm here . . . once again. This is getting ridiculous." Picking up my phone, I punch the on button and nothing happens. "This can't be. It worked two minutes ago. What's wrong with it now? Maybe if I move around the room, I can get coverage." Walking around and holding it up in the air, no luck. "Damn. When will Jerry be back? Let's see . . . I came up here about two o'clock, worked a little while in the office, and then a little bit in here. It could be about four o'clock by now and Jerry thought he would be back about this time. I shouldn't have long to wait. Hopefully, Shadow will show him where I am again.

"Wait a minute. Who else is here? How in the hell did this door shut? I had it propped open. Someone had to actually slam it; there's no way it would just do that by itself. Who wants me out of the way to look around? What are they looking for? Maybe the necklace I found in here? It's a good thing I didn't just leave it in my room or out in the open."

Going over to the other soft leather chair, I reach under it and find the box Jerry put there. Clumsily sliding it out, I open it. The velvet cloth, necklace, and painting are still there. "Whew. Am I glad to see these. But, if this is what they're looking for, they might come back to check out this room. Only, I'd be in their way. That can't be a good thing." Putting everything back in the box, I slid it back under the chair.

"Okay, what do I do now?"

Chapter 48

"Think. If someone comes in here what do I have I can use to defend myself? Of course, if they have a gun, I'm out of luck." Frantically looking around the room, on one side I see empty shelves where Jerry took the computer hard drives. The two, soft chairs sit in another corner with a small table between them and the two file cabinets sit along another wall. "Damn. Nothing here to help me. Not even a painting, but wait a minute. There is a statue on this wall shelf. Geoffrey only glanced at it so it must not be of any real value. I was going to look more closely at it before, so guess now would be as good a time as any."

Taking it off the shelf, I notice it's more of a bust and not an actual figure. I don't recognize the face; in fact it's almost a caricature and doesn't even look like a real person's face. It's rather small and not at all heavy as I turn it around in my hand. "I can see why Geoffrey ignored this piece. It's ugly. Probably wouldn't even make a good weapon." Looking at the bottom of it I see an indentation. "This whole piece is weird. My thumb fits into this open spot. Oops."

As I place my thumb into the indentation, the top of the head twists to the side. "What the hell? Did I break it? Well, I'll be. There's a hole in his head. Why would you have a statue with a hole in it?" Tipping it I notice something inside and reach in with two fingers. It's a tight fit but I manage to get a grip on a slippery piece of paper and pull out a small wrapped bundle. "What do we have here?"

Setting down the statue, I carefully unwrap the paper. "Wow. What the heck is this? It looks like a dagger or a fancy letter opener." About four inches long, the blade is only about half of that. Inlaid stones and pretty, enamel paint cover the handle. "This is amazing and beautiful. I wonder what it was used for and why is it here? Why would he hide this? Again, did he just steal it and was waiting to display it?"

I turn it over in my hand and run my fingers along the blade. It's sharp but not deadly sharp. "I bet it's a letter opener. Even though it's fancy, it's dainty. Probably for a lady. I'm going to keep it out and put the statue back together. I can't wait to show it to Geoffrey and tell him where I found it. Hmm. There are other statues downstairs. I wonder if they hide treasures, too. Once I get out of here, I'll have to check."

Turning the top of the head back in place, I set the statue on the small table and stick the letter opener in my pocket. I also check my cell phone and see it still isn't working.

"Okay, now back to figuring out how I'm going to get out of here. Jerry has to be coming back soon, I hope. But, what if he walks in on whoever locked me in here? What if they kill him and no one finds me? How long can I survive in here?

"Stop it. Get a grip. I can't think negative thoughts. Stay positive, Marta; form a plan."

I don't think my positive self-talk is doing any good. Sitting down, my thoughts range from helpless to Grandma to Reid to Clark and back to helpless. "What on earth did we get into, Grandma? How long would this have continued had Reid not died? Who is his assistant and who was helping him? Why hasn't Clark called me? Okay, I need to think logically.

"His assistant has to be someone in the area. That only makes sense. But, why hasn't he shown up at the estate? Or, is he the one breaking in? That would make more sense, because he wouldn't have to actually break in. He'd have a key, gate code, and everything else necessary to just come on in. Reid's assistant can't be

Priscilla because she is the first one to mention he had an assistant, and I don't think she had it in her to lie about that.

"If the assistant is the one breaking in, it would also make sense the dogs wouldn't bark to alert anyone he was here. They'd be used to him. Hmm. They didn't bark at Special Agent Mark. You don't suppose he's his assistant? No, that doesn't quite fit. He doesn't live here. Who else didn't they bark at? I don't think they barked when Tom, the locksmith came. Could he be Reid's assistant? Did they bark when Sandra and her team were here or at Jerry? I don't remember. I don't have any idea who they bark at and who they don't anyway.

"I understand cats a lot better. So, let's see who Shadow doesn't like. There's Mark . . . he didn't like him at all. Or, Priscilla. He likes Jerry and Geoffrey. He likes Sandra but I seem to remember he didn't like the guys with her. Oh dear. So what? I can't figure it out and does it really matter? I can't do anything about it right now anyway."

Sighing, I lean back in the chair and rest my hand on the statue bust sitting on the table. "I wish you could talk or at least had a working phone in your head." My other hand rubs my coin necklace. "I need help, Grandma. Now would be a really good time." Nothing happens. "Okay, so maybe this coin doesn't really save me."

With a loud bang, the door to this room crashes open and once more I scream.

Chapter 49

Jumping to my feet, I'm shoved back down in the chair by a large man wearing a ski mask.

"Okay, I'm done searching this place. Where is it?" I'm staring into the barrel of the handgun he's pointing at me. I can't see his face and even though his voice is muffled, I know I've heard it before.

"I have no idea what you're talking about. If you would just tell—" Lights explode in my face. His fist slams into my jaw and my head jerks back. Sharp pain instantly gives way to throbbing, dull pain and I gingerly touch my jaw. I blink to clear the stars I'm seeing all around.

"Okay, bitch! Tell me where it is and I'll leave you alone to die in peace."

Afraid of another hit, I tentatively look up at him. Why can't I recall that voice? Holding up my hand, I take a breath and whisper. "Don't hit me, please. Let me ask a question. Okay?"

Roughly grabbing my arm, he jerks me to my feet. "One question. Then, you tell me where it is. Got that?" He's at least a foot taller than me. His grip on my arm is painfully tight.

I nod, try to steady myself, and try to move away from his grip. It doesn't work. "Don't think of running either. I'll shoot you in the back. I don't care. I just want what belongs to me." I nod again just as we hear someone talking. It sounds like the person is entering the office.

"Gino, where are you? Did you find the woman?" Another man, also wearing a ski mask and waving around a handgun, walks into the inner room, coming close to me. His weapon is aimed at my face. "Good. Now we can make her talk."

Just as I think things can't get any worse, the first man lets go of my arm, shoves me to the floor, turns to the second man, and shoots him in the head. That man falls to the floor, lifeless, his handgun dropping beside him. Then, my captor bends down, grabs my arm, and yanks me to my feet. "I told you I don't care who I shoot. You're next unless you tell me where it is. Got it?"

Nodding once again, I hold up my hands to shield my face from another blow, and then drop them to my side. At the same time, my mind is trying to figure out so many things. Who are these men? What do they want? Did the other one call this man Gino? Where have I heard that name? What do I tell him? My hand brushes my pocket and I remember the letter opener. Can I use it somehow? I step toward my captor and at the same time reach into my pocket with my right hand.

"I'll tell you where it is." Looking at him, I motion toward the outer office with my left hand. "It's out there."

In the split second his eyes leave me to glance out at the office, I lunge at him with my meager weapon. I slightly misjudge and end up stabbing him in the arm. He swings around takes aim at my face with his fist. I duck and the handle of his gun grazes the top of my head. More pain as I hit the floor.

"Okay, this is enough. No more distractions. I want it and I want it now. It's mine. I'm giving you one last chance." His foot comes in contact with my side as I try to roll out of his way and feel something hard under my thigh. It's the other man's handgun. He reaches down, hits me once more, and then pushes me with his foot. Desperately hoping I can pick up the gun and point it, I reach under my leg, grab the weapon, and aim in the direction of my captor. I fire until I can fire no more and then collapse back down in a heap. I'm deaf from the commotion and my body is in pain. Stars amid a red haze. I'm losing it.

Something wet is on my face. Fur is brushing up against my hand.

Looking up through swollen eyes, I see a wolf and hear a meow. And then I hear Jerry before I pass out.

Chapter 50

Trying to open my eyes is hard. Trying to move . . . even harder. I'm not sure I can speak, but I try. "What happened? Where am I?" My feeble voice sounds like squeaks to my ears. Something is hammering inside my head.

Jerry comes into fuzzy view. I blink. "Marta, take it easy. We'll explain everything once you are fully awake. Right now, I want the doctor to see you again." He has a hold of my hand and I hear him talking to someone else.

An older man in a white coat appears and shines a really bright light into my eyes. "How are you feeling, young lady? You gave us quite a scare. Nothing is broken. But, you'll have a lot of pain and probably some major headaches in the next couple of days. I gave Jerry some pain pills for you and I want you to take them. No heroics, okay? These will help. You can tell everyone what happened later. Right now, I want you to get some more sleep. Okay? I'll come and check on you tomorrow. For now, rest." He gives me some water with the pills.

I start to ask a question but my mind is still fuzzy and I feel like I'm falling into a hole. Then, darkness.

Coming up out of the darkness takes time and I slip back and forth, finally emerging. My mouth feels like I've spent a month in the desert, my head feels like I have a full drum core playing a march inside my forehead, and I'm disoriented. Where am I? What's going on? I attempt to sit up as Shadow sits by my head and purrs. "Am I glad to see you, Shadow? Where am I?"

"Well, we're all glad to see you, Marta." Jerry has moved to my side. "Here, let me help you sit up. Take it easy. You've been out for almost two days."

"Two days? What?" I start to ask another question as my memory slowly returns and some events start coming back to me. I look around and see I'm in my bedroom suite at the mansion. Shadow moves from my head to my lap and I rub his ears. He purrs.

"He sure is glad to see you. He likes me, but always comes in here to sit with you. It's hard to get him to leave."

I take a deep breath and feel some pain in my side. "Whew. That hurt." I feel the bandage on my head. "How bad was I hurt, Jerry? Wait a minute, where is the guy that attacked me?"

"If you're up to it, I've made dinner. You should eat something. We can either go downstairs slowly or I can bring it up to you. Then we both need to talk about what happened. Okay?"

"Let's try going downstairs. I feel like I've been in this bed for weeks." Jerry helps me stand and puts a robe on over my pajamas. Shadow follows us as we slowly leave the bedroom and enter the hallway. Walking is easier than I feared, but I lean on Jerry as the room still spins. "Whoa. Is that a wolf?" Sitting outside my door is the largest, fluffiest critter I have ever seen. He stands up, looks at me with huge gold eyes, and nudges my hand with his snout. When he licks my hand, his grin reveals some serious teeth. Shadow just stands and looks at him without so much as a growl or hiss.

Shaking my head, I look at Jerry who chuckles. "Nope. Meet Milo. He's part of the story. I figured since he and Shadow took care of you, you wouldn't mind if he guarded your room. They get along just fine." Jerry points to Shadow and Milo.

I look at Shadow, who is now standing by my leg. He's not even fluffed up at this massive critter. "What's the deal, Shadow? Don't you know he's a dog or a wolf or a wolf-dog?" Shadow walks over to Milo, brushes up against him, and starts down the hallway. Milo follows.

"Actually, Marta, I think Shadow is the alpha here and Milo is happy to be in his pack. Milo truly has the husky pack mentality and somehow accepts Shadow as the leader. It's funny."

We all finally make it to the kitchen where Jerry helps me sit, feeds both animals, and takes a wonderful smelling dinner out of the oven. "Wow. I am really hungry. It seems like weeks since I last ate anything."

"Well, it's been at least two days and you've had some serious pain meds. Your last pill was six hours ago so I don't think you should have any wine. Are you in any pain now?"

"Not bad. Things hurt, my head only pounds a little, and my side aches when I take a deep breath. But, it's not unbearable by any means. Who gave me the pills? Did I see a doctor here?"

"Yes, I had a doctor come here to take care of you. He gave the okay for you to stay here and not go to a hospital. He's come several times in the last two days. I gave you the pain pill when you woke up about six hours ago."

"Wow. I don't even remember waking up until now. I must have really been out of it."

"Yeah. Pain and injury will do that to you. Let's eat and then we can talk about what happened. Okay?"

"Sure." I take a bite of some delicious lasagna and it hits me. "Wait. Weren't there men here wearing ski masks? Pieces are slowly coming back. Did I kill one of them?"

"Let's finish dinner and then we can go back upstairs. I'll give you all the details I know. Okay?"

Chapter 51

We finish eating, Jerry picks up the dishes, and we slowly head up the stairs to the office with Shadow leading the way and Milo bringing up the rear. I can almost see things as they happened and I hesitate before entering the office.

"Marta, are you okay? You don't have to do this. We can go somewhere else."

"No, Jerry. I'm fine. I want to see everything. I also want to make sure the door to the inner office is fixed so it never shuts again." Looking at it I see the door is no longer there. The doorway has been remodeled so it looks like an entry way to another part of the office suite. "Wow. Who did that? It looks like it's always been that way."

"Thanks. I did that while you were sleeping off the meds. I figured you wouldn't mind and I tried to make it look like it was supposed to be that way. The new owners can use this back area for a reading nook or storage or whatever. You'll never have to worry about being shut in there again."

"Thank you so much." We walk to the inner office, which has been completely cleaned out except for the two comfy leather chairs and a couple of small side tables with the fake bust-like statue sitting on one. "This looks great. The whole office looks better and I'm sure it will be much better for Sandra to show.

Speaking of Sandra, I should call her. I think she was supposed to get back to me with a time to show this to a client."

"While you were out of it, you did receive a couple of calls from her and I answered them. She is coming tomorrow, but first we need to talk about that. Are you ready to go through everything that happened?"

"Sure, Jerry. You go first."

Jerry helps me into one of the chairs while Milo sits down, filling the middle of the floor. Shadow jumps onto my lap while Jerry takes the other chair. "Okay, here goes. As you know, I went to Interpol in London with all of the equipment and files. They're unraveling more of Reid's life and his connections. He had developed quite the plan over the last couple of decades. As soon as they have everything sorted out, they'll come here to brief us on the events.

"I have left a few messages with Clark to fill him in on things. Interpol has also tried to contact him about the missing piece of Reid's team; the inside man in law enforcement. Reid relied heavily on him for information and no one can figure out that part of the puzzle yet. They're assuming he's an Interpol agent or possibly FBI, but don't have a good lead on him right now. Anyway, all this took a whole lot longer than I originally thought it would, so I was quite delayed in getting back here. I called and left two messages on your cell phone telling you I would be late."

"Really? I never received those. Is it because I was stuck here in this room?" I pull out my cell phone and see that it works just fine. But, no messages. "Why wouldn't it work when I was locked in here?"

"The door was lead lined and that could be why your phone had trouble. However, no one has any idea why Reid would have a lead lined door. It's bizarre. But, it's gone now. I'm not a phone expert, but I don't understand why you wouldn't receive the messages. We'll work on that later. It's not important now.

"To continue, it was kind of late when I made it back here and I had a bad feeling before I even came through the front gate. For some unknown reason, I had taken a back road from the village.

About a quarter of a mile from your front gate there were two cars parked at the side of the road. I went right past them and then turned back around to check them out. One was a very nice white Mercedes and one was an expensive Audi, both locked. They certainly didn't look like they had car trouble, but no one was around them.

"In my mind, though, something wasn't right, and when I cautiously approached the front gate, I noticed it was open. No dogs came running and I was afraid all three had escaped. Milo loves to run. I decided to park outside the gate and approach on foot. No sense alerting anyone with my truck."

While Jerry is talking, I'm nodding and putting pieces together in my mind. I let him continue.

"The front door was shut but not locked. I quietly pushed it open and that's when I heard gunshots."

Chapter 52

"The gunshots I fired?"

"Yes, Marta. I ran up the stairs toward the office and saw quite the scene. Now, you tell me what happened and then I will finish."

Taking a sip of my water and rubbing Shadow's ears, I fill Jerry in on my day. "I had come in here to finish organizing the last two file cabinet drawers so we could move the cabinets out of here. Once again I had my back to the door when it slammed shut. And, I do mean slammed. I even had it propped open so I knew someone had to physically shut it. I was worried whoever was here wouldn't find what they wanted and would come back here to deal with me.

"That's when I sat down to think and picked up this odd statue. I remember thinking Geoffrey didn't give it a second glance, so it couldn't be valuable. I started fiddling with it, found an indentation in the bottom where my finger fit, and the top of his head moved. Like this." Picking up the statue, I insert my finger and the head opens. "Wait. Did I have something in my hand when you found me?"

"Yes, you did. Was that what you found in this head?"

"Yes. There was a piece of paper wedged in this hole and I pulled it out. When I unwrapped it, I found a fancy letter opener.

At the time, I wondered why on earth Reid would hide that in here. I figured he stole it and was hiding it until he could display it. Do you have it now?"

"Yes. Once Interpol dusted it for prints, I put it in my bedroom. I'll get it when we're done here."

"Interpol was here?"

"I had to call them when I found you and everything else. Please continue."

"Okay. I remember thinking about Grandma, then about Reid and his assistants, and then it hit me that Ted, the new guy on Sandra's team reminded me of someone. I was just going through people in my mind when the door crashed open and this guy came in. He had a ski mask on and a handgun pointed at me. He wasn't happy and told me he wanted what was his. He said I had something that belonged to him.

"When I tried to ask a question, he hit me in the face. I think I asked him not to hit me again and that's when another man with a ski mask came into the office. Oh, I remember. The second man called the man in here with me Gino. Isn't that the name of Reid's assistant?"

"Yes, it is, Marta. Go on."

"Well, Gino turns and shoots the other guy in the head. It was just so simple to him. He turned and shot." Shaking my head I close my eyes. "I can see it clearly. It was horrible."

"Have a drink of water and take your time, Marta."

"I knew I had to do something or I'd be next. I figured he was going to kill me anyway, so I might as well fight. I had put the letter opener in my pocket and I pulled it out when I told him what he wanted was out there. Briefly, he turned to look out into the office where I had pointed and I lunged at him with it. I only stabbed him on the arm and that made him madder.

"I think this is when he knocked me down and kicked me. I was hurting everywhere by then. But, when I fell down I somehow landed near the dead guy and could feel something underneath me. When it dawned on me it was the handgun from the now dead man, I knew I only had one option left. I pulled it out from under my leg and started shooting. I had no idea if I hit anything. I was slightly disoriented at that point and my ears were ringing with the noise.

"That's when I remember the wolf and Shadow. I heard you and then nothing until I woke up in bed.

"Fill in the rest, Jerry. Please."

Chapter 53

"Okay. I heard the gunshots and had no idea what to expect. I got up here as quickly as I could, but Milo beat me up here. No idea how he got in or what he thought, but he practically ran over me on the stairs. He went right to you and Shadow followed him.

"The man you were lying next to was dead, shot through the head like you said. The other man was dead, shot several times in the chest. Good shots, by the way. You were a mess but Milo and Shadow were trying to comfort you. I think Milo growled at me so apparently you are now his responsibility."

"Who were the men and what were they looking for, or do we know?"

"As soon as I stabilized you, I called Interpol while doing a quick search around the house. No one else was here but your bedroom was a mess again. One of the statues in the den was smashed."

At this, I sit up and point to the head on the end table. "Was there anything in it, like in this one?"

"Nope. But, maybe that's what they thought. As soon as I knew you needed more medical attention than I could administer, I called a physician friend of mine who lives in the village. We put you in bed and I cleaned up your room, as he tended to your injuries. Since he determined they were bruising and nothing broken, he allowed you to stay here. You were out of it the entire time. He gave me strict instructions what to do and he stopped here twice a day to check on you and change your bandages."

"Wow. Thank you. I must remember to thank him, as well."

"You can do that when he stops later tonight. After we took care of you, Agents Collins and Green from Interpol arrived and figured out who the dead guys were. They also took care of their cars. After piecing things together, we now know the first dead guy, the one shot in the head, is your locksmith. His name really was Tom and he had a record a mile long. He was pretty much a petty thief who Reid apparently took under his wing. Like others, Reid fine-tuned his stealing abilities and helped him graduate to murder. Just your basic hired gun. We still don't know how or why he arrived here so soon after you contacted the legitimate locksmith company. Interpol is working on that.

"The man he called Gino, was indeed Reid's assistant. The thing is he used fake credentials to join Sandra's team as Ted. Apparently, he figured he could steal whatever they were after by working here on the inside. Somehow the two of them must have had a falling out in order for Gino to shoot Tom. Or, maybe Gino never intended to share with Tom. We'll never know that part. Are you getting tired?"

"No, I'm still okay. I want to get the rest straight in my mind." The front door bell rings and Jerry looks at the monitor.

"I gave the front gate code to Dr. Smythe. That's him at the front door. I'll go let him in and you stay right here."

Nodding in agreement, I pull out my phone and call Clark. Once again, voice mail. "Clark, I have to assume you are extremely busy and maybe even working undercover. We have had too much activity here. Two men, one apparently worked for Reid and the other one was Reid's assistant, broke in and tried to kill me. I'm okay and it's a long story. Jerry is helping me. We aren't sure what they were after and Interpol is still involved. Call when you can. Marta."

Just as I put my phone back in the pocket of my robe, Jerry enters. With him is a tall, handsome man with the face I kind of remember seeing. "Marta, it's so good to see you up. How are you feeling? I'm Dr. Gregory Smythe, a friend of Jerry's. Please stay seated."

"Dr. Smythe, it is so good to meet you. I can't thank you enough for taking care of me."

"That's what I do. And, please call me Gregory. Now, let's take a look at your injuries and your head. How are the headaches? How about your ribs? Are they still sore? You took quite a beating, young lady. When was the last time you had a pain pill?"

I answer Dr. Smythe's questions and look to Jerry for the answer about the pain pill. "I gave her a pain pill about seven hours ago now. She was semi-awake and having a hard time resting."

I smile at Dr. Smythe. "Even though I feel like I've lost a heavyweight battle, I don't really have serious pain. Just a small headache and my ribs hurt if I breathe too deeply."

"That's good. You're going in the right direction. Why don't we try ibuprofen for now and if the pain is too great in a couple of hours, you can have one more pain pill. Okay?"

*C*hapter 54

We all talk some more as I learn Dr. Smythe knows Jerry from his days at Interpol. When he gets ready to leave, he tells me he'll be back tomorrow. When I tell him it probably isn't necessary, he gives me a stern look. "Maybe not, but I'll be here anyway. Try to have a restful night. And, be sure to take a pain pill if you need it. One more day will be okay."

Jerry walks him to the front door as Milo moves closer to my chair. Shadow is back on my lap and for some reason he isn't hissing at Milo. Strange, but I'm okay with that.

"Do you want me to put Milo outside, Marta?"

"No, I kind of like him here."

"I'm sure it's okay with him. I am going to take him out for a couple of minutes and check on the other two. I'll be back in a few."

With Jerry and Milo gone, I scratch Shadow's chin. "I am so glad all that is over with, Shadow. I do wonder what they were after, however. I need to ask Jerry if Interpol has any idea. I also need to ask about the letter opener. I'd like to see it again."

Jerry and Milo come back in and Jerry is talking on his phone. "Yeah, Peter, that is odd. Unless they wore gloves the whole time. Let me know what else you find. Talk to you later."

"What was that all about, Jerry? What has Interpol found? Do they know what the two guys were after or what I'm supposed to have?"

"Marta, they haven't figured out what they wanted. I'm going to get the letter opener I put in my room and we can look at it together. It's possible it's that or the necklace. And, when the agents had the cars towed to their lab, the lab couldn't find any finger-prints. None. Everything had been wiped clean. That's what Peter was calling me about. They don't understand that."

"Even if they wore gloves, wouldn't there be some prints, Jerry?"

"That's exactly what puzzles them. Especially since both cars were wiped clean. I'll be right back with the letter opener."

A couple of minutes later, Jerry brings it to me and we both inspect it. "Do you think this was a letter opener? I wonder if it's old."

"It looks like it, but I'm not an art expert. Too bad Clark isn't here."

"Oh, speaking of Clark, I called and left a voice mail. Do you think he's undercover and that's why he can't be reached, Jerry?"

"It could be. I haven't heard from him, either, and it's begin-ning to bother me." Jerry is examining the letter opener under the light. "Look at these markings, Marta. Any idea what they mean?"

Shaking my head. "No, sorry. They kind of look like initials, maybe the goldsmith who made it. Wait, let me take a photo and send it to Sam. Maybe he's seen something like this before. I should also ask Geoffrey about it to see if it's valuable or has been reported stolen." Taking out my phone, I snap a quick shot and forward it to both Sam and to Geoffrey. "Jerry, I am getting tired. Is it okay if I turn in for the night? I don't think I need a pain pill, though. The ibuprofen seems to have dulled my headache. I'm sure I'll be better in the morning."

"Of course, Marta. Let me help you to your room. Why don't you take this with you in case Sam contacts you with some ques-tions about it?" Jerry helps me up and hands me the letter opener, which I put in the pocket of my robe.

Milo and Shadow follow us down the hall. Shadow jumps in bed and Milo takes up his position right outside my door. "Ahh. My protectors. Night, Jerry."

Chapter 55

In spite of weird dreams where I'm being chased and hiding under beds, I wake rested with no throbbing headache. My ribs feel better when I stretch. Looking in the mirror, however, I am shocked. Apparently, I hadn't seen my reflection in a mirror in several days. Bruises on my face, chest, and side are lovely shades of purple mixed with even uglier shades of yellow. Refreshed from a warm shower, I make my way downstairs, where wonderful scents lead me to the breakfast room. My faithful companions follow along.

"Shadow, you and Milo must be best friends by now. This is so odd. I had no idea you would like a dog, especially one this huge. But, he does seem to follow you everywhere."

Jerry greets us and lets Milo out the back door. "Sit and eat. I'll feed all the animals while you enjoy breakfast." He's poured a cup of coffee and a glass of fresh squeezed orange juice, and set a plate with a huge slice of quiche in front of me.

"I'm starving and this looks amazing. Thank you."

I'm about finished when he comes back into the breakfast room. "Sleep okay?"

"Yeah, even though I had a bunch of strange dreams. I feel pretty good now." My phone rings and I see it's Sam. "Sam, it's so good to talk to you. You won't believe what's been going on here." I fill him in on everything.

"Marta, are you okay? What were they after? Have you talked to Clark? Clark's friend is still there with you, isn't he?"

"Yes, Sam, I'm okay. A little sore but getting better each day. I keep leaving messages for Clark but no response. Jerry and I think he must be undercover and can't return our calls. And, I have no idea what they wanted from me. Interpol is working on that." Then I ask what he knows about the letter opener.

"Well, Marta, I did a little research. I can't be real sure until I actually see it, but I think it is important. The initials on it appear to be a monogram but I can't really tell from the photo."

At the mention of monogram, I remember the necklace. "Sam, I completely forgot in all the craziness here. The necklace we found has a purple velvet cloth with what I think is a monogram and a small oil portrait. I need to take better photos and send those to you as well. Maybe they all fit together or maybe Reid stole them from the same person."

"I have the necklace photo you sent earlier, but send me photos of the monogram and I'll do some more research on it. Nothing is showing up on any bulletins about stolen artifacts that resemble the letter opener or the necklace, though."

"I'll have Jerry get it out and I'll send more photos in the next few minutes. Thanks, Sam. I'll be in touch."

Jerry has been listening and tells me he'll go get the necklace so I can take some more photos and send them to Sam. He comes back with the box. "This thing would withstand a direct hit from a bomb, I think. It's solid. I wonder why he used this and I wonder where he got it. If I had to guess, I'd say the box is quite old."

We remove all the contents, take photos, and send them off to Sam. "I'm not sure where we should keep it for now. But, I guess we won't have to worry about it being stolen now that Reid's men are no longer around. I'll put the box in your closet with your suitcases so you can take it to Venice with you. Is that okay?"

"Great idea, Jerry." I finish my coffee as Jerry comes back into the breakfast room. He's on his phone. "Really? Let me talk with Peter or Thomas. Oh, I see, that's why they had you call me. Yeah, I can be there in about a half hour. Tell them I'm on my way. Thanks."

"What was that all about, Jerry?"

"Agent Bridgestone, from the Interpol office where Thomas and Peter work, called me. I don't know him, but he was calling for Thomas. Apparently, there have been some major developments and they want me to brief me with what's been going on. They think they know who the mole is in law enforcement; the one helping Reid stay one step ahead of everyone on every investigation."

"Why can't they come here?"

"I asked and apparently they have too much information to bring here. Do you want to come along?"

"Not really. I think I'll contact Sandra to see when she's showing this place and then take a nap. I might also visit with Geoffrey about the letter opener to see if it shows up on any of his bulletins. It doesn't bother me to stay here, as long as I have Milo and Shadow to protect me."

"Not a problem. They'll both stay in the house and I'll only be gone a couple of hours. Okay?"

"Sounds good to me. When do you leave?"

"I need to leave right away, but I won't be gone all that long."

Chapter 56

Walking upstairs to the office after Jerry leaves takes time as I'm still a little sore. I make a call to Sandra and find out she's showing the estate tomorrow about 11 o'clock, which works for me. We don't talk much about Ted other than she has been told he wasn't a legitimate antique appraiser or a realtor and that he used false credentials. She thinks he was arrested and I don't tell her any different for now. I let her know Jerry and I can be in another part of the house for about an hour. Then I make a call to Clark and leave yet another voice mail, talk to Geoffrey and give him a description of the letter opener, and finally make another call to Sam who is working on the letter opener and necklace with Henri.

Milo and Shadow follow me from the office to my bedroom. "Whew, guys. I'm tired. Who knew walking up stairs and making phone calls would wear me out? I think I'll take a quick nap and see if I have the strength to start making dinner before Jerry gets back." They seem to understand as Shadow jumps up on the bed and Milo sits by the door as I crawl under the covers. My phone is on the bedside table and I take out the letter opener to see if I can decipher the initials on it. "Sam seems to think these mean something. I should have brought the purple cloth with me to compare the initials on it with these, but I'll get it after my nap." Drifting off, I tuck the letter opener under my pillow.

The next thing I know someone is calling my name. "Marta. Wake up, Marta. I need for you to wake up."

I'm groggy as I open my eyes and try to focus. Mark is standing at the foot of my bed. "Mark. What are you doing here? Who let you in? Is Jerry home?" I shake my head to clear out the dreams and cobwebs.

He's grinning at me. I sit up in bed and start to get up. "Marta, please stay where you are." His stern voice is more of a command than a request.

"Mark, what's going on? What's wrong?" I move my pillow.

"Oh, Marta. We need to talk. You have something that belongs to me and I need to get it back. Clark told me you had an awful fight with Gino, but you didn't give him what he wanted. That's okay. It doesn't belong to Gino anyway. It belongs to me." Mark is now pacing near the bed, waving his arms around, his eyes are narrowed. All of a sudden, I'm fully awake and I'm also afraid. I try to look around to figure out where Milo and Shadow are, but I don't see them.

"Mark, it's good to see you. If I have something of yours, I would be more than happy to give it back to you. Just let me know what it is. Okay? You say you talked to Clark? How is he? Did he tell you he'll be here shortly?" I need to stall. How long have I been asleep? When is Jerry due back here? What can I do? Where are Milo and Shadow?

"Marta, you really don't know, do you? Clark's not coming to your rescue. He doesn't even know what's been going on. He thinks you're in Venice and you don't need him. Who knows, he may even have a fatal accident in the near future." With that Mark laughs, sits down in one of the chairs, and looks at me with a scary stare, his eyes piercing right through me. I shudder and try to compose myself.

"What do you mean, Mark? What kind of accident? Why on earth would Clark think I'm in Venice? I haven't even talked to him in several days. I leave him voice mails so he does know what's going on here. He leaves me messages with his itinerary. I know he'll want to see you when he gets here. We can all reminisce about

San Francisco." Mark is grinning as I am rambling. He's not buying anything I've said.

"Marta, I need to explain some things to you and then you will give me what is mine. I worked for all those years and I deserve it. The others were idiots, anyway. They didn't believe in facts, like we did. They had no brains. All they saw were dollar signs, not the power. Even then, they messed everything up. It's just as well it ended like it did for them. Less things for me to explain." Mark stands up and walks around my bedroom, muttering and gesturing in the air. I'm not sure exactly who he is talking to or what he's talking about. He's not really making any sense. I'm halfway listening while forming a plan in my mind. If I just knew where Milo was.

Mark stops and turns to look directly at me. "Okay, Marta. Quit pretending. Your grandma knew all about it and now you know what I'm talking about. Give it all to me right now and I won't make you suffer." The pupils of his eyes are black. He's breathing heavily. What does Grandma have to do with this, I wonder, but no time to ponder that. I scoot up in bed, trying to get away from his stare. It dawns on me the letter opener is here right here, as I tuck my hand under the pillow and feel the cool blade. Mark is walking closer to the bed. I need to buy some more time.

"Mark, where is Milo?"

"Who? Oh, you mean the dog that was sitting in the hallway? I lured him outside with some meat and bones. He's not coming to save you. Now, quit stalling and give it to me." As he takes two more steps towards me he pulls a handgun out of his jacket pocket. "This can be quick, Marta, and you won't feel a thing. Just tell me where it is. NOW!"

As quick as lightening, several things happen. I don't have time to think.

He takes one more step, now standing closer to me, and aims the gun at my head. I pull the letter opener out from under my pillow to somehow defend myself once more with this meager weapon. "One last chance, Marta." He comes within an arm's length of me, sees the letter opener, and laughs.

From out of nowhere Milo growls and jumps on Mark's back, pushing him toward me. The letter opener finds a direct hit in Mark's chest. He grabs his injured chest, drops his gun, and rolls onto the floor screaming. Blood is everywhere.

Chapter 57

I scramble off the bed as Milo gets between Mark and me. Shadow hisses and jumps at Mark's face, claws out. He scores a hit as Mark tries to grab him. Seeing Mark's gun, I go for it the same time he does and he gets to it before I do. "You're going to pay for this, Marta." He's gasping for air and blood is dripping onto the beige carpet.

Milo growls showing all of his teeth, Mark aims the gun directly at him, and I hear a single gunshot. Afraid to look at Milo, I can't take my eyes off Mark. His entire body jerks back and he lands with a soft thud on the carpet. A single hole is the middle of his forehead. More blood. Milo is licking my face and Shadow is still hissing at a now lifeless Mark.

In slow motion I turn toward the doorway and see a solitary figure. Then it registers.

"Clark. What? How? Are you—?" Darkness envelopes me.

The next thing I know, I'm sitting on the floor with Milo on one side, Shadow on my lap, and Clark holding my hand. Coming to, I look up at Clark. That's when we hear noises coming from downstairs and Clark touches my arm. "Shhh. Be quiet and stay here. I need to see what's going on. Okay?" His gun in his hand, he steps to the side of the doorway and looks out. He's just about to step through when I hear Jerry.

"Marta, are you okay? Who is here with you?" Then silence. Clark is now standing with his back to the interior wall, signaling me to stay quiet, and his gun ready. Jerry comes to the door with his gun drawn, looking around, and sees Mark on the floor. Looking at me, I nod my head, and he enters the bedroom. "What's going on?" He kneels down by my side, petting Milo on the head.

Clark steps away from the wall. "Hey, there, are you alone?"

With a speed I didn't know he had, Jerry picks up his gun, whirls around and takes aim at Clark. I'm speechless. Milo growls and Shadow seems to echo his growl.

Jerry speaks first. "Clark. You scared me. What are you doing here? Are you the one that took out this guy?" He points to Mark lying on the floor.

Clark lowers his gun and nods. "Jerry, are you alone?" Jerry nods, they both lower their weapons, Jerry tells Milo to sit, and then they both look at me. Shadow has moved to my lap as I sit on the floor. Jerry notices the blood all over my hands. "Marta, are you hurt? Where did he get you?"

Coming out of my daze, I look at my hands. "I don't think it's my blood, Jerry. I think it happened when the letter opener pierced Mark's chest."

"What? How did the letter opener get in his chest? Wait. Before you answer that, let's get you cleaned up and you can both tell me what happened." He looks at me and then at Clark.

About a half hour later, I'm showered and dressed. Coming out of my bathroom I see Agents Collins and Green in my bedroom with Dr. Smythe and another man who is putting Mark in a green body bag.

Dr. Smythe comes to me and asks me to sit down. Taking out his bright light, he looks first into my eyes, then examines my head. "My dear. You have to quit scaring me. Are you feeling okay? Did you get hurt in all of this?"

"I think I'm fine. I was taking a nap and the next thing I knew Mark was here with a gun. He didn't hit me or anything, though. We struggled a little but Milo did most of the work in taking him down. Then I think Clark shot him. Thanks for coming to check on me."

Agent Collins comes over and speaks to Dr. Smythe and me. "Hey, Doc, thanks for coming. Marta, the coroner will get this body out of here and then we all need to go downstairs where we can find out what happened. Doc, I'd like you to stay too, if that works."

I glance at where Mark was laying and see the blood stained carpet.

Chapter 58

Thirty minutes later we are all assembled in the den; Jerry, Clark, Agent Collins, Agent Green, another man I don't recognize, Dr. Smythe, and me. Milo is by my side, sitting on my foot and Shadow is on my lap. Someone has made coffee.

Agent Collins takes the lead. "We need to walk through everything that happened here in the last few days. We also need to understand issues Clark has been having. I believe we'll all have a better understanding of Reid's life and how his system worked. I also believe we each have an important piece of this whole puzzle and we'll find out how everything fits together. Is that okay with everybody?"

We all look at each other and nod.

He continues. "I'll start and ask each of you to fill in your part as we go." He looks at each of us. "Doc, I asked you to stay in case Marta needs you." Dr. Smythe smiles at me.

"Interpol is always investigating art thefts, especially when they involve murder. Paintings get stolen, important archeological artifacts get misplaced, and so on. In this case, a pattern of art thefts was developing about 15 years ago that led us to Reid. We couldn't ever catch him directly, but things just kept pointing to him. When we looked more closely at him, we were confused at first. He was, emphasis on was, a legitimate collector with seemingly endless wealth. However, nothing pointed to where he acquired that tremendous wealth. We still aren't completely sure but have some ideas.

"Then, about six or seven years ago the thefts became more brazen, more often, and were accompanied by murders. All with the same MO; slit throats. No idea why his pattern changed. Interpol and the FBI were so close to catching him on several occasions, but we always managed to be one step too late. It was like he had eyes on all of us. We figured he had someone on the inside, but could never find the mole. Believe me, we tried. We laid traps and still no luck.

"Marta and Clark have seen some of the pieces here he stole from collectors all over the world. Some of those people had accidents, some were murdered, and some he apparently just stole from. No idea how he decided what he wanted. Until Marta's grandma's music boxes became the hot item for him and he came after you, Marta, in Italy nearly a year ago. We are still missing the 'why' piece of that puzzle. We know he was your father, Marta, but that just can't be all there is to it. We're still digging there. Why did he want those music boxes so badly?

"Now, to this place and the recent events. Clark you have been briefed on Tom and Gino and them being here. We figured Reid had an assistant, then Priscilla mentioned one, and Marta and Jerry confirmed it with some files they found. That was Gino. He's been doing most of the dirty work for Reid. When there was something Gino didn't want to do, he farmed it out to Tom. They worked as a pair on many of the thefts and apparently on the murders as well, according to the fingerprints we finally were able to get from their bodies.

"Everybody with me so far? Questions?"

We're all silent. "Okay, I'll continue. Someone has been leaving threatening messages on Marta's phone, telling her to give it up. Right, Marta?"

"Yes."

"Then, there were some break-ins here with those same words written on your mirror." I nod as he continues. "Finally, Gino and Tom came here looking for whatever it is they wanted. Sam, in

Venice, has been receiving the same messages on his phone but no break-in to my knowledge. Is that correct, Marta?"

"Right. But, a jeweler Sam knows was murdered with his throat slit. Is that connected?"

"We think so and are working with the authorities there on a couple of things. Now, today, Special Agent Mark Smith, with the San Francisco Police Department, came here. But, he was here before, wasn't he Marta?"

"Yes. First, he said he was on vacation and then he said he wanted to date me because we hit it off in San Francisco. I still have no idea what he was talking about. And, he gave me the creeps. Oh. I'm positive he and Priscilla knew each other. That was always weird. Did they know each other? And, where is Priscilla in all of this?

"Priscilla is in custody, as an accessory. Now, back to Mark who came here today. You were left alone when Jerry came to the office, right? Please fill us in on what happened here, Marta."

Chapter 59

"Certainly. After Jerry left, I made some phone calls and decided to take a short nap. I was still a little tired from all the activity and the attack the other day. I didn't take any pain pills, so I knew I wouldn't be asleep for long. Shadow was with me and Milo was guarding the door. Something woke me; I think it was Mark talking to me."

I look down at my hands as I try to remember how the conversation went. "He kept saying I had something of his and that the others shouldn't have it, or something like that. I asked him what I had and told him I would be happy to give it to him. He just kept telling me I had it. I remember him saying something about Grandma. Like she knew what it was or something. He wasn't making any sense.

"He brought up your name, Clark, and it seems like he indicated you were dead or had an accident or something along that line. He said you weren't going to help me. I was trying to stall him with questions. He wouldn't let me get out of bed and told me to stay where I was. I kept hoping Jerry would be home soon.

"When I didn't see Milo and asked about him, Mark told me he gave all the dogs some meat outside. He said Milo wouldn't be able to help me. I asked him some more questions as he walked around the bedroom, but he was getting more agitated by the minute. That's when I remembered the letter opener. I had been looking at it before I took a nap, trying to decipher the initials on it. I was tired and had just slid it under my pillow instead of putting it away.

"When my hand touched it, I figured it was the only weapon I had. I knew he was going to kill me but I was going to try to hurt him as well. He came at me with his gun pointed at my head and told me I had one more chance to give it to him. That's when Milo pounced on him from the rear, and he stumbled and fell toward me. I had the letter opener in my hand and he fell on it. There was blood everywhere. I'm not sure where it pierced him, but it didn't kill him.

"He dropped his gun and I was going for it. Shadow jumped on him and clawed him but he managed to grab the gun before I could get to it. Then I heard a shot and I thought he killed Milo. I was so scared. I looked at Mark, saw the hole in his head, and looked at the doorway. That's when I saw a figure but didn't realize it was Clark for a couple of seconds. It just didn't register right away. Wait a minute, aren't you supposed to be in Dubai and undercover or something?" I look at Clark.

Agent Collins nods and points to the man I don't know. "Marta, this is Agent Seth Gray. His specialty is technology, especially tracking phone calls and more." Agent Gray gets up and shakes my hand. "Nice to meet you."

"Likewise, I think."

"Let me fill you all in on exactly what Agent Gray, Seth, does. Clark you're already in on this, but we need to clear up the issues for everyone else.

"Marta and Jerry, we now know you've been leaving voice mails for Clark and others. Right? Sorry to listen to your calls, but we'll explain why we did. Clark started noticing about a week ago he could not leave voice mails for either of you. He would call and the phone would ring once, then hang up. No option to leave a voice mail. He couldn't text, either. Is that right, Clark?"

"Yes. At first, I just figured you were busy, Marta, and probably had your phone off or your mailbox was full of voice mails. Then, I remembered I had hotel security look at my phone shortly after I arrived in Dubai as it wasn't working quite right. I wondered if those events were connected, but I didn't contact Seth until a few days later. By that time, I couldn't leave messages for you or Jerry. I even tried Sam and no luck there, either.

"Seth dialed into my phone, did his thing, and realized someone had put a bug in it. I don't have all the particulars and Seth probably doesn't want to give up any secrets, but bottom line . . . your phones, Marta and Jerry, and mine were being monitored."

Jerry and I look at each other and both speak. "Who would do that? Why?"

Agent Collins looks at us and then at Seth. "Fill them in a little more, please Seth."

Chapter 60

"Sure thing. When I looked at Clark's phone, I noticed some unusual activity that shouldn't be there. I probed further and found what I was looking for. Someone who knew what they were doing had placed a sophisticated bug in the software on Clark's phone. It directed it to act like it was placing outgoing calls but in reality, nothing was working."

I interrupt. "I kept leaving voice mails on Clark's phone, though. Or, at least I thought I was. And, we did talk once or twice."

"Yes, you were leaving voice mails. They were received by Clark's phone and then forwarded on to someone else. Clark had no idea he was receiving voice mails from you or Jerry, or anyone else for that matter. But, others could hear them and hear what you were up to. And, the calls that actually went through? Those were because Clark just happened to be calling you at the very same time. It was pure luck."

Clark's turn to interrupt. "Marta and Jerry, I couldn't understand why I had no calls from you to let me know how things were progressing here. That's when I knew I had to contact Seth."

Seth continues. "We unraveled everything yesterday and found out who was listening. I'll let Peter continue." He looks at Peter.

"First of all, remember we knew there was a mole, some-one who was helping Reid? We knew he had to be pretty high up and able to monitor several different agencies, because all of us were having the same trouble pinning anything on Reid. We had focused on Interpol and then on the FBI. Those made the most sense. When Seth contacted us with the information he found on Clark's phone, we knew we had our guy." Peter pauses.

I interrupt. "Is that why you called Jerry to come to your office?"

"Ah. I forgot to mention that part. No. We didn't call him. That call was made to look like it came from our office. There was no call, no agent Bridgestone. The reason the bogus call was made was specifically to get Jerry out of here. This guy wanted you alone. I guess he figured you wouldn't go with Jerry."

It's dawning on me who Peter is talking about.

"Continuing on. Jerry leaves and you don't go with him. The plan is in place. Apparently he waits until he doesn't hear you mov-ing around or making noise and he figures he can sneak up on you. He feeds the dogs and waits for you to wake up.

"What he doesn't know is that we know about him and have for almost two days. Clark is on a plane here but we don't want to call you or Jerry as we don't know who is listening and we don't want to alert anyone else. Things got a little bogged down or Clark would have been here before Mark arrived. And, we figured Jerry was here anyway. It was only after he arrived at our office that we knew you were in trouble.

"Backing up a minute, no one had looked at an agent with the SFPD, didn't even think to look. When we poured over the photos Jerry brought from Reid's computer, we kept seeing Mark in odd situations. Once we pinpointed Tom and then placed him with Mark, things started falling into place.

"By now, Clark had called his contact at the SFPD and learned even more about Mark. He was under suspicion regarding the death of his partner, Lynne Greystone. Recently, they were also looking at him as some surveillance equipment was missing, but no one knew where he was. And, this is important, they recently discovered a tie to one of the murders that had to do with the music boxes. That one just surfaced. We were just learning all of this and finally fit the pieces together. Then, you know the rest. He came here to get something from you. As near as we can tell, the three of them, Tom, Gino, and Mark, were all after the same thing. Partners, perhaps?"

"Well, he did say something like the other two didn't deserve it. I didn't quite follow him but maybe that's what he was referring to. I thought he was just rambling, but then again maybe not."

"You're probably right, Marta. Now if we just knew what they were after."

Chapter 61

My phone rings. "It's Sam."

"Marta, why don't you put him on speaker and I can talk to him as well." Clark comes to sit by me, moving Milo off my feet.

"Hello, Sam."

"Hello, Marta. How are you?"

"Sam, we have so much news to tell you. In fact, Clark, three agents from Interpol, and Jerry are all here and we have you on speaker phone. But, you called me, so you go first."

"Hi, Clark. This is good as I have several things to tell you. And, it's good that everyone can hear what I have to say all at the same time. Clark, I left some messages for you. Did you receive them?"

"No, Sam, but that's part of what's been going on here as well. Tell us your news first."

"Okay. Marta, I've been looking into the necklace you recently found. I enlisted the assistance of Henri here in Venice. Even though we only have photos, we're both positive we know where it came from and how long it's been missing."

"Oh dear, Sam. I was afraid it was stolen. I knew it. I just knew he stole it and hid it away. Okay. Let us know who we need to return it to."

"Well, wait a minute. Marta, I hope you're sitting down. Reid did indeed steal it. He stole it from your grandmother."

"What? How? When? Are you sure? Why wouldn't she have told me? What on earth?"

"It's a long story. Here goes. You know we figured out your grandmother descended from a royal family and we thought we had it narrowed down to either northern Italy or Austria. Thanks to Henri, he and his connections traced her family back to the Venice area, based on those old family records she had and using some family names we came across. It would be your great, great grandparents who were wealthy people in early Venetian times. We're talking wealthy. The tiara we found, your grandma's music boxes, her jewelry, and more can all be pinpointed to the area and the time frame. This necklace you found was handed down to the oldest boy in the family to use as a wedding gift for his bride. This family practice started out in the early 1800s, as near as our records show.

"Now, based on additional records, we know your grandmother had it when she left Italy for America. Bear with me here. The great-grandfather of one of Henri's jeweler friends is the jeweler who made it. Or maybe it was the great, great-grandfather. At any rate, because your grandmother was an only child, it stayed with her. See, the thing is it was always registered with the jeweler's shop when it was passed down to the next generation. The old records they kept were amazing in helping track this."

"We're with you so far, Sam. But, that doesn't mean Reid stole it. Wouldn't she have passed it to him to give to my mother? Isn't that what she was supposed to do?"

"Ah, yes. However, she takes it to America, apparently has it with her until Reid is getting ready to get married, and then it gets stolen before she can give it to him. Or, at least that's what the jeweler's registry says. There is a very clear note in there from her reporting it was stolen. We have no idea if she reported it to any US authorities or not. And, that's the last mention of it. Until now, that is."

Clark is nodding to the Interpol agents. "Peter and Thomas, do you think Interpol has records that date back that far. Or, is that not something they would even have on their radar?"

"Good questions, Clark. We can check but I'd bet we'll find nothing."

"Sam, this is Clark. Do you or Henri think Reid stole it from her? Any indication of that?"

"No, Clark, we have no idea who stole it. She only says it was stolen. You might want to check with the local law enforcement wherever she was living at the time."

"Sam, that would be Minnesota. Grandma came to the United States to marry Grandpa and they lived in Minnesota after that."

"Sam, this is Jerry. Even if the local police had a record of the theft at that time, apparently they never recovered it as it was here in his house. He must have had it for a long time. What I don't get, is why he had it stashed away here and not displayed with the rest of his stolen treasures. I guess it's possible that Mark and the other two found out about it and thought they could steal it from Reid. Thieves often turn on each other and this may have been the case with the necklace. Or, did he just plain forget about it? I highly doubt that as he didn't seem to forget anything."

"Jerry, I agree about all of that. I honestly don't know why it would not be on display, unless he knew the others were after it. Marta, where did you find it?"

"In the bottom of a file cabinet in a locked room. It was a secure room with a substantial lock, though. Still, it was quite hidden. And, the box it was in was also quite substantial. Did you find out anything about the initials on the purple cloth or the painting that was with it, Sam?"

"Not yet. We're still looking at those and I'd like to see that in person. I just thought you'd like to know about the necklace, Marta. It belongs to you now. Since it's from your grandmother's side of the family, I assume you want to keep it. In any case, Henri will appraise it for you. Keep it safe for now. Okay? Speaking of Henri, he's also looking into your coin some more. Pedro had just started uncovering more about it. We know it's not just a coin. It has some special meaning as well. Keep that safe, too."

"Thanks, Sam."

Chapter 62

Hanging up from Sam, Clark is the first to speak. "Good news about the necklace, Marta. Even though Reid apparently stole it, at least it belonged to your grandma. Now it is yours. It was odd of him to hide it, though. Who knows why he would do that? It seems to me it would be quite the piece to show off. Unless, of course, it is the piece the others were after. I guess it would make sense to keep it out of view. I do wonder if he knew they wanted it before he died. All unanswered questions."

The coroner comes in, has a lengthy conversation with Agent Collins, and then leaves. Two other men wait and leave with him. Agent Collins announces, "The coroner's preliminary time and cause of death relate directly to what all of you have said. There will be no investigation into his death. Interpol is looking into any next of kin and will take care of reporting to them if they find any. The cleaning men have cleaned the carpet and it is almost dry. All of the blood stains were removed. The new owners will not be able to tell anything, other than they have clean carpets in that bedroom. There will be nothing in any news media about this. Mark's cause of death will be reported in the San Francisco paper only as he died while on vacation in England. The San Francisco Police Department are looking into his private computers, residence, and personal life as well as what he had at work. They are also investigating him for the murder of his partner.

"For all purposes, we will be closing the case shortly on all of this. Does that meet with your approval, Clark?"

"Yes, it does. Thanks. I think Marta, Jerry, and I can handle what's remaining here. Once Marta has this place sold and all the remaining items taken care of, we'll all be finished with Reid, his thefts, and his murders. We can all move on with our lives. Sound good, everybody?"

With a puzzled look on my face, I'm absently petting Shadow. Every now and then Milo rests his nose on my leg. Clark looks at me and can tell I still have unsettled questions. "What is it, Marta? You look like something isn't quite right. Do you have more questions we haven't answered yet? "

"No, not really. I understand everything that happened here and I believe we are finished with everyone connected to Reid and his thefts. My questions are more about Grandma and Reid. What did she know and why didn't she tell me? Was she protecting me from him? Or, did she not really know what he was doing? Maybe she genuinely thought he died in the plane crash, just like he wanted everyone to believe. I guess there's no point wondering what the real truth is now, though. We're done."

Jerry is looking at me. "Didn't you tell me your grandma kept journals, Marta? You don't suppose she made notes about him, do you?"

"Jerry, what a great thought. Even though I thought her journals were about growing up in Italy it is possible they're more than that. I only glanced at them once or twice and knew I wanted to sit and read them thoroughly when I had more time. Now, I'm wondering if she documented anything that would help answer my questions."

Clark nods at both Jerry and me. "Are they back in San Francisco, Marta?"

"No, I had them shipped to my place in Venice before I came here. I knew I was going to be spending a few weeks in Venice and thought that would be a good time to really delve into them. I guess I'll have to wait until I get there. And, that's okay."

Agents Collins and Green have been talking to each other privately and now get ready to leave. Agent Collins addresses all of us. "We're going to get back to the office now and clean up all the paperwork. Clark, we'll let you know what the SFPD finds out about Mark and if he has any next of kin. For now, as far as Interpol is concerned, everything is wrapped up. Stay in touch, all of you, if anything else develops. Okay?"

Dr. Smythe stands and comes over to me. "Marta, how are you feeling? I know you didn't take any more blows but the stress sometimes causes reactions to injuries. Are you okay? Any headaches?"

"Thanks for asking, but I seem to feel okay. My head hurts a little right here, but other than that, I'm fine. I know my bruises must look amazing by now." Dr. Smythe chuckles and looks at the spot I was referring to on my head.

"That's where you took the worst blow. It will be sore for a while. You should take ibuprofen regularly for a few more days but I don't think you need the pain pills. It will get better. As for the bruises, it's probably a good thing you're not entering a beauty contest. They would clash with your outfit."

We all smile at that and he leaves shortly after the Interpol agents, telling me he will stop in tomorrow evening to check on me.

Chapter 63

Shadow leads the way as Clark, Jerry, and I make our way to the kitchen with Milo bringing up the rear. "It's really interesting how Milo seems to do whatever Shadow does, Jerry. I never would have thought my cat would put up with a dog, especially one as large as Milo."

Jerry smiles as he starts dinner while Clark opens a bottle of wine. "I didn't ask the doctor, but I would think you could have a glass now that you aren't on the pain pills, Marta."

Clark makes a toast as we raise our glasses. "Here's to putting the issues of the past week behind us and moving forward without any more catastrophes."

Jerry smiles and adds his own toast. "Here's to uncovering the truth."

Shaking my head, I look at Clark and Jerry. "Has all of this really happened in only a week? Just think, a week ago I didn't even know you, Jerry. Clark, can we really put everything connected to Reid to rest? And, do we really have all the answers?"

"Marta, I would hope so. What else is left to uncover? Sam is working on the necklace, the letter opener, and the monogram or initials. But, that's more for information purposes. We know all of that belongs to you. Once you get this place sold, you'll be rid of anything connected to Reid. I'm assuming there's nothing here you're going to take with you. Other than the necklace and letter opener, that is."

"Right. I want nothing else from this place. And, I hope it sells tomorrow when Sandra brings her client here. She said they were very interested and didn't want her to show it to anyone else."

"Marta, have you decided what you want to do with the wine? Are you going to include that in the asking price?"

"Jerry, you can have as much of it as you want. I'll take some to Venice and Clark, you can take what you want. I'd just as soon have most of it gone and then I won't have to think about it."

"I'll take a couple of bottles, but you have some expensive wine in there."

"Jerry, please take more than a couple of bottles. You enjoy it and after all, Milo saved my life. I'll buy him a steak and you get the wine."

We finish eating and Jerry is looking through the wine as Clark's phone rings. After a lengthy call, Clark hangs up telling us he has information from San Francisco. "Let's relax in the den and I'll relate what the SFPD just told me."

Once we're all settled, Clark begins. "SFPD continued to look into Agent Mark's past. He was already on their radar for several issues over the past couple of years but they couldn't put all the pieces together until his partner, Agent Lynne, was killed. Mark's prints were discovered on her suicide note, but since he was the first agent to go to her home and find the note, it wasn't a red flag at first. Until, that is, they did some more investigating and did not find any of her prints on the note. Curious, to say the least.

"Now when they searched his home again, they found parts of items stolen from the SFPD, records on his computer, and a key to a safe deposit box. That's when the rest of the story fell into place. It seems he kept detailed records of all transactions he did for Reid. They're thinking these were for insurance in case he was caught. Everything, including all activity, is recorded for the past 10 or so years. The FBI and Interpol will be looking at these notes more closely as he mentions others in law enforcement that assisted him along the way. This is a major breakthrough for all of law enforcement. Once their investigations are complete on everyone associated with him, the case will be closed. And, that's good news for all of us."

Jerry looks at me and breathes a sigh of relief. "Clark, that's fantastic news. I'm sure our former colleagues at Interpol and the FBI are finally glad to have something go their way. For you, Marta, you can rest easy knowing everything with Reid is coming to an end."

"Clark, did Mark have any relatives, a wife, girlfriend, or even friends?"

"Not that they can find. According to his employment records, he was adopted, never married, and pretty much a loner. They're thinking Agent Lynne must have been on to something concerning him and his illegal activities and that's why he killed her."

"Poor woman. I liked her."

"Yeah, I know. Me, too. On a lighter note, what time is this place being shown tomorrow, Marta? Do we need to leave during that time?"

"Sandra will be here at 10 o'clock and told me we could stay in case anyone has questions. I guess we can all hang out some- where. After all, it is a big place."

"Clark and Marta, I'll stay here tonight but Milo and I will get out of your way in the morning before they arrive."

$\mathcal{C}$hapter 64

After breakfast, Jerry and Milo prepare to leave. "Marta, it has been quite the adventure. I'm so sorry things happened to you when I was supposed to be here to protect you."

"Don't even think about that, Jerry. Remember, Milo is the one who came to my rescue. I have no idea what Shadow is going to do now that he doesn't have a follower." I give Jerry a big hug and bend down to hug Milo and get a big, sloppy lick from him. "Please come to Venice or San Francisco to visit me. I mean that. I'm not sure Milo would do well on the plane, however. I guess I could always come here to visit him . . . and you, of course."

Jerry laughs as he encourages Milo to jump into his truck. Milo looks at Shadow and me, and I swear he smiles as they drive off . . . all teeth.

Clark and I make sure we stay out of the way when Sandra and her clients arrive and start to look around. "Marta, how long are you staying here once this is sold? I need to get back to Dubai to wrap up things there, but could meet you in Venice after that. It shouldn't take more than a week. Would that be okay with you?"

"Clark, I completely forgot about Dubai. Thank you for putting that aside to come here. And, most definitely I would love for you to come to Venice. We could finally spend time together."

"I would like that, Marta."

"Great. I really can't wait to get out of here. Geoffrey is coming later today with his moving people to take everything for the auctions, private sales, and to his clients. Did you know those Picassos are worth what he told me? Of course, you know. That's your business. Still, I was floored at what his clients are willing to pay me. And, if Sandra's clients don't want the crystal, he has a buyer for all of it. Whew. I can't believe the money some people spend on things.

"Speaking of that, where do you suppose Reid acquired all of his money to buy the paintings and things he actually paid for?"

"That's a good question. We might never know the answer. Oh, here comes Sandra. Maybe we should move to another part of the house."

Sandra comes into the breakfast room where Clark and I have been having coffee. "Marta, my clients would like to purchase your estate. I have all the paperwork, they have a certified check for the down payment, and an agreement with their bank to transfer the remaining amount into your bank. Do you need to visit with your attorney or may we proceed today? Clark, you are welcome to be in on the transaction."

"Whoa, Sandra. That was quick. Do they have any questions? Did they accept the asking price? I'm stunned."

"Marta, no questions, yes to the asking price, and they love it. They've been quietly looking at estates since they acquired some money after one of their parents died. Apparently, he had developed a patent on something, sold it, and made a huge amount of money, which he invested. They want to move as quickly as possible. I always check out my clients before I show something of this magnitude as I don't want to waste anyone's time. They are legit. It's up to you. Want to sell today?"

"Yes. Let's do this. Clark, please stay here. I might pass out!"

Three hours later, all the paperwork is signed and notarized, money has been transferred, logistics with the dogs and other items that will stay has been finalized, and I'm speechless. Possession will be in two weeks in order for the money transactions to clear and in order for Clark and me to get moved out. They give me a big hug as they leave, telling me they love the dogs and the entire estate. "Come visit us when you're in England. And, be sure to bring your lovely cat. We're so glad we were able to purchase this place. No one has ever seen it and it is exactly what we've been looking for." With that, they leave, Sandra picks up everything she brought with her, and heads out the door.

"Well, Marta, it's been a pleasure. I'll stay in touch and you do the same. This has been quite the day, huh?" She gives me a big hug. "Thanks again for choosing my firm and good luck with everything. Let me know when you leave for the last time. The clients have the gate code and you can leave the keys in the box by the front door. Will that work?"

*C*hapter 65

Over a quick lunch, Clark and I discuss our plans for leaving just as Geoffrey arrives with several moving trucks and vans. "Great timing, Geoffrey. We just finalized the sale of the estate about an hour ago. I now know what needs to stay. Your client who wanted the crystal will be disappointed as it's staying. The furniture in the large dining room is also staying. Everything else goes, except for Clark's and my personal items in our bedroom suites."

"Marta, that's fantastic. Congratulations. I knew it would sell quickly as exquisite as this place is. Any chance I can make you a deal on your cat?" He grins at me.

"Nope. Not a chance. Sorry. He's my friend and protector."

Geoffrey gives me a shrug and a frown. "Okay, we'll get to work then." He directs the men to various rooms and they work quickly and efficiently. Clark and I head to our respective bedrooms and pack our own things. We both leave in the morning; me on Mario's jet to Venice and Clark to Dubai.

A few hours later, I'm packed as Shadow and I make our way downstairs. The heavy, old box with the necklace, monogrammed purple cloth, small painting, and letter opener are tucked safely in my bags.

Clark is talking with Geoffrey and I wander around the now empty rooms. "Wow. Your men are almost finished. I forgot to ask about bedroom furniture and items Clark and I will be using tonight and tomorrow. How do the new owners deal with these things?"

"Marta, I will leave my card on the kitchen counter with a note telling them I am available in case they need something disposed of or decide they want to move something out. Would that be okay?"

"Great idea, Geoffrey. Thanks."

Shortly, everything is packed up, the moving men are gone, and Geoffrey is ready to leave. "This has been such a pleasure, Marta. Your pieces are listed on two different estate sales and money will be deposited in your account tomorrow for the Picassos. I have all of your contact information and will be in touch with you. Here is a certified report of what I took today. And, if you decide you don't want this gorgeous cat . . . let me know." He's holding Shadow, who loves every minute of the attention.

We exchange good-byes as Geoffrey leaves and then Clark and I wander back into an empty house. "Marta, let's celebrate all the events of the day. Since we both leave fairly early tomorrow, it will be an early night for me. Is that okay?"

"Perfect. At least we have food for dinner and some fantastic wine. I've boxed up what wine I'm taking and I'm glad Jerry took as much as he did. I figured you wouldn't be able to take any with you. That leaves a few bottles and I'll just leave them with a note for the new owners to enjoy. What a day. Let's make a toast to ending this adventure."

"And, to keeping it ended. Okay, Marta?"

Chapter 66

Early the next morning, we are at the private airport not far from the estate. Mario's plane is waiting for me and an Interpol plane is waiting for Clark. We bid each other good-bye, for now, knowing Clark will be coming to Venice in about a week.

"Marta, take care, and tell Mario and Sam hello from me. Let me know what you find in your grandma's journals and I'll let you know if the SFPD or the FBI has any more info on Agent Mark. I'll see you a week from tomorrow."

"Clark, I can't wait until you come to Venice. We can have some time to ourselves, have a normal conversation, and explore the city some more. Thanks again for everything."

A few hours later, one of my favorite cities comes into view as we descend into the Venice airport. "Well, Shadow, time for you to adjust to this city and our house here once again." He meows from his cat carrier.

Mario greets us as we enter the private jet terminal. "Marta, so good to see you. But what is wrong with your head? Are those bruises? What happened?"

I fill him in on all the events as we head to my home, the small palace I inherited from Grandma, and tell him Sam is working on some newly discovered items for me. "I'll show those to you once we get there. They're quite spectacular." We chat some more as he catches me up on what's been going on here in Venice, at the vineyard I co-own in the Dolomites, and with the renovations that were being done at my home here.

"Everything is complete at your home, if you are satisfied with the work. I can't wait for you to see it. You will have to let me know what you want to do while you are here. I thought we would take a couple of days and go see Lorenzo and your vineyards, if that's okay."

"Yes, I was planning on visiting him. And, I had Grandma's journals shipped here before I left San Francisco. I want to read them to find out more about her life as a young girl. Now, though, I want to see if she makes any mention of Reid. It's possible I'll learn a little more about him and why he did all the things he did."

"Good thought. If she spent time writing in her journals as a young girl and then once she lived in America, she may have continued writing into her adult life as well. But, don't get your hopes up. You may never know any more about him. Are you okay with that?"

"Positively. I was mainly hoping to find out why she originally had the necklace, when it was stolen, and what her thoughts were about that. We also need to talk to Sam to see what he found out about it. Why don't we all get together for dinner tomorrow night? I will have had time to at least skim the journals. I can read them more thoroughly later then. You and your wife and Sam could come to my place. Would that work?"

"Sounds like a plan. Are you sure you want to cook?"

"Absolutely. I can't wait to try out my new kitchen. That's the part I'm most excited about." Our water taxi pulls up to the stop near my home and we unload my luggage and Shadow's carrier. He's not overly pleased about the boat ride and is sulking in the corner. "We're just about there, Shadow."

Once we arrive at my home, Mario takes me around and shows me the renovations while Shadow finds some sunlight and begins to groom himself. I'm pleased with everything and thank Mario for overseeing it all.

"I'll let you unpack and see you tomorrow, Marta. You can call Sam to let him know you're here."

Chapter 67

Once I've unpacked, I settle down with a glass of wine and start reading Grandma's journals. The first ones are definitely related to her life here in Italy as a young girl and then as she learns the art of pastry making from a chef here in Venice, who was Mario's grandpa. Thinking I will read those again later, I look at the next ones and see they refer to her meeting my grandpa in the hospital during the war. No mention of the necklace yet. Touching my coin necklace, I look to the Heavens. "Will I ever find the answers, Grandma?" My phone rings and I see it's Sam. "Sam. Good timing. Can you come to dinner here tomorrow night? I have the necklace and letter opener, along with the monogrammed purple cloth."

"Marta, that works for me. I just want to give you some more news about your coin, the one I made into a necklace for you. Are you ready to hear some incredible news?"

"Sure. What's up?"

"Your grandmother's family, dating back several hundred years, was influential in this area. The coin you have was their family coin and it was used as a symbol of royalty and of importance. Many important families had coins similar to that one and would use them for trade, or when their daughters were married, or other significant life events. We're pretty sure the face on yours is that of the family's patriarch and possibly a Doge at one time. This is a rare coin. Only two others like it exist and they are in museums. There are dozens of legends surrounding these coins. But they are just that . . . legends. Henri and I don't really believe it has any special powers or anything. But, he does know that certain coins were influential when an important family wanted to acquire more land, another palace, or some other kind of wealth. They opened the door, so to speak. So, it did have its own kind of powers during that time frame. Keep it safe. I don't mean put it in a safe. Wear it and remember your grandma. Pretty special, huh?"

"Oh my goodness, Sam. Do you really think it's okay to wear or should I donate it to a museum? I mean, it hardly seems fair for me to wear it when others could enjoy it. I could always have you make another necklace using one of Grandma's gemstones. That might be better. I wouldn't have to worry about anything happening to this one, then."

"That's up to you, Marta. I'd be happy to create a new necklace for you and you'd still have your grandma with you as you wore it. Think about it and don't make any hasty decisions. Whatever you decide will be great. Now, I need to run, but I'll see you tomorrow night."

I go back to reading Grandma's journals as I think about what Sam just told me. "Shadow, what should I do?" He doesn't answer, so I move to the next pile of journals. Time passes as I learn more about my grandma and piece together her life as it relates to the stories she told to me. I don't even realize it's dark outside as I pick up the last pile.

These start with her and Grandpa in Minnesota, where he's farming and she's creating pastries. No mention of any children or the necklace yet, but I keep reading. That's when I learn more than I ever thought I would.

"No way. Now, everything makes more sense, Shadow." Putting down the last journal, I can almost see how events unfolded. "No wonder. I can't wait to tell Clark, Mario, and Sam. Shadow, let's go to bed. I know what I'm going to do with this coin." Touching my coin necklace, a warm feeling comes over me and I can't help but think it's Grandma approving of my decision.

Chapter 68

The next night we're all gathered at my place; Mario and his wife, Suzie, Sam, and me. Clark and Jerry are both on speaker phones. Except for Clark, we all have a glass of wine from Reid's cellar.

"First, I want to make a toast to good friends. I would not have made it through all of this without each one of you. Thanks so much.

"Now, I want to fill you in on what I read in Grandma's journals and then tell you what I'm doing about my coin. This is kind of a long story, so please bear with me." Taking a sip of wine and a deep breath, I relate what I read.

"I'll start with her journals from Minnesota, after Grandma and Grandpa were married. They were approached by someone they knew from the university, asking if they would adopt a baby. Apparently, that person knew of a baby whose parents were killed in an accident. The baby had no other relatives. So, Grandma and Grandpa adopted him. This child was Reid." Sam and Mario have the same look on their faces and I hear Clark mutter.

"Grandma and Grandpa had no other children, either before or after the adoption. Grandma makes a few notes about Reid's childhood, but nothing unusual or out of the ordinary. Just typical first child stories. Then, when he is in college she makes several entries saying she is concerned about some issues that keep

211

happening. Reid always seems to be in the middle of these. In one instance, there were some accusations from a professor and some test files were missing. Another time, Reid was questioned about a missing piece of pottery from a museum collection. Nothing actually pointed directly to Reid, and she mentions later that those investigations were dropped. But, Grandma must have had serious suspicions to make detailed notes about them. At one point she writes that he scares her with his ruthless attitude and she wonders if he will make it through college.

"Her next journals concentrate more on her pastry, recipes she's developing, and spending time with me. She has a couple of journals dedicated to those subjects, and I will have to read them better at a later date. For now, I wanted to find out what I could about Reid.

"Moving forward, he graduates and gets hired as an assistant professor at the university and once again controversy surrounds him. Now, this part is interesting. He meets my mother, who was a little older than he was, and they get married after knowing each other only a month. Grandma loved my mother and she writes that she is bothered by this quick marriage. This is where it gets better for my peace of mind. My mother had been married before and had me. Her husband, my biological father, was killed in Vietnam. So, I am not related to Reid at all. I am so relieved to know that."

"Marta, that is such great news for you. But, what did Reid do that upset your grandma? Do you know?"

"Thanks, Clark. Yes, Grandma's notes actually become even more detailed about Reid and the things he did. I'll give you the short version. She calls them shady dealings, specifically mentions some thefts that are connected to the university, and then writes he has come into a great deal of wealth. When she asks him about that, he brushes her off. Apparently, she asked him about this wealth on several occasions and wrote about each of those times in her journals. She even makes a couple of notes in the margins of some pages saying she needs to get to the bottom of this.

"Grandma then notes that she found out Reid was once again under investigation, apparently several times, by the university but she doesn't know exactly why. At one point my mother came to Grandma with her own concerns about Reid, about missing artifacts, and about their increasing wealth. That's when Grandma did some digging into his actions and she writes she doesn't like what she's finding. Then, more accusations, and immediately after the last accusation from the university is when he and my mother's plane went down and they both supposedly died. Grandma writes that the timing is strange. She even hires someone to look into the accident for her, but nothing is discovered.

"Her next entries have to do with her coin and her necklace, the one we found in Reid's mansion. She describes the coin and gives a detailed account of how and why it was kept in her mother's family. This account matches with what you and Henri found, Sam. According to what she writes, it is a special coin and it does have certain powers . . . but not really saving people like one legend says. She writes that it is the key in growing their estate and their family's worth and that it is worth far more than its gold content. At one point she says it will stay hidden and when the time is right, she will tell me about its history.

"Next, she writes about the necklace we found and how it relates to our family history. Again, this all matches with what you found as well, Sam. She says she made a decision to give the necklace to my mother to pass down to me. But, she is adamant that Reid not get his hands on it. She even had talked to her attorney as she wanted a legal document stating that. That was just before they died.

"After the news of their deaths, she goes to get the necklace out of her special place and discovers it is missing. She hadn't looked at it for several months, but does write that Reid knew where she kept it hidden. He didn't know the story behind it, only that it was spectacular and worth a great deal. She reports it stolen, has strong suspicions that Reid took it, and figures it is lost somewhere. She and Grandpa went through all of my mother's and Reid's things and didn't find it. They did find some valuable artifacts that belonged to the university, however. When she returned them, she learned of many more missing pieces. But, she never found the necklace in Reid's things.

"She mentions she wants to get back to Italy to find out more about her grandmother's history. She realizes it's more important than she once thought. I can't seem to find those journals about that part of her history. I don't know if they are missing, or lost, or what, so I'll look for them later.

"Now, these next journal entries are kind of weird and scary. Fast forward to me living in San Francisco where she writes about her visits to me, things we did, and people she met. Then she writes the next entries in black marker . . . almost like she wanted someone to notice these. She is positive she saw Reid in San Francisco when she was visiting me and reminds herself to warn me about him. According to her notes, this happened on more than one occasion. She worries about the fact that he is still alive and she is concerned. Then, one entry is rather chilling. She has vowed to protect me, no matter the consequences. I'm not quite sure why and not sure what consequences she's referring to. She doesn't say. But, she does write that the men she keeps seeing are not going to harm me. I know she was completely lucid up until the day she died, so I'm sure she didn't imagine any of this.

"Her last journals are written shortly before she died when she mentions her necklace again and hopes it will someday be recovered. Then, she writes about the coin once more. It's pretty much the same thing as before but she writes about it again, so it must have been on her mind. She says she hid the coin in the bottom of the jewelry box to keep it safe. She refers to it as her crown and says it was meant to be revered for the power it holds.

"The very last entry is about Reid and the coin. She had a disturbing phone call about a month before she died and detailed that call in her journal. Let me read what she wrote; 'I'm positive the phone call and message was from Reid as his voice was always quite distinct. He told me he already has the necklace and knows about the coin. He said he intends to get the coin one way or another and people will be hurt in the process unless I give it to him now. He mentioned my music boxes as he rambled on about having what he deserves and that my life and Marta's life are both in danger if we get in his way. Then, he called me an old woman not worthy of the kind of wealth and power he's going to have. I must warn Marta. These are serious threats. We're in danger. He's quite mad.'

"That's it. That's the last entry. Her deathbed warnings must have been about Reid, the coin, the necklace, and his state of mind. Or, at least that's my take on it."

Laying the last journal with the rest, I lean back and Shadow jumps on my lap.

Chapter 69

"Whew. It's amazing to have these journals from your grandma, Marta. What peace of mind this must be for you." Mario has raised his glass to mine.

"Thanks, Mario. I am relieved by the fact I'm not related to Reid. At the same time, I'm saddened that Grandma had to go through all of this. I wish I had known about him. I also wish I had understood her warnings to me. They're still a little confusing in my mind."

Clark offers the most plausible theory about Grandma's deathbed warnings. "Marta, your grandma was probably going to fill you in on the whole story at some point before she died. Her health issues just happened so fast, she didn't have time to explain it all to you. Hence, the cryptic warnings. But, she knew her journals, music boxes, and other treasures would be making their way to you. And, she knew you, Marta. You wouldn't just ignore them. She was special to you and her things would be just as special. She knew you would find out the truth somehow."

"Thank you, Clark. I can almost see her figuring out how to get everything to me without anyone else knowing what she was doing. Especially after I read her concerns about seeing Reid, the message he left her, and the fact that she thought he was mad. She really was protecting me from him. In fact, she had probably always been protecting me from him. And, for that, I love her even more."

"Marta, you mentioned your coin and the plan you have for it. Do you want to share that?" Sam is scratching Shadow's chin and Shadow is purring.

"Oh, I almost forgot, Sam. I am donating it to the museum here in Venice, in Grandma's name. I thought that was only appropriate. I do want you to make another necklace for me, though. One I can wear to remind me of my fabulous grandmother."

"Of course, Marta. I would be delighted."

Clark and Jerry hang up and everyone else gets ready to leave. Mario reminds me we have a trip to my vineyards in the Dolomites in a couple of days and Sam gives Shadow one last head scratching before he leaves.

"Thanks to all of you for helping me get through this. Grandma would have appreciated all of your help."

Good-byes are said and Shadow and I head upstairs to bed. "Well, Shadow, it's been quite a journey, huh? Now, we can really relax and enjoy our home here in Venice. Things are better for all of us. Goodnight, Grandma." Shadow purrs like he knows what I'm talking about.

*E*pilogue

A week later Shadow and I are sitting on the terrace of my palace in Venice, waiting for Clark to arrive. I'm drinking a glass of bubbly, tasty Prosecco from Lorenzo's and my vineyards and Shadow is on my lap, purring. "I'm glad I had time to read the rest of Grandma's journals, Shadow. Her life and her family's history were pretty amazing. I do wish we could have explored that history together, but I guess it wasn't to be. And, I am glad I now know all about Reid. Grandma had come to the conclusion he turned into a horrible person. I'm just glad she didn't know how many murders he was associated with, though. Finally, I understand why she wasn't all that upset when he was supposedly killed in the plane crash. I think secretly she was glad I wouldn't have to be around him any longer.

"I'm so glad I decided to donate Grandma's coin to the museum here with her name as the donor. The curator was absolutely delighted to have that piece of history to share with everyone. That makes it all the more special for me. He was also glad to have Grandma's family necklace on loan as well. I did the right thing and I know Grandma would approve.

"And, Sam did a wonderful job of creating another necklace for me with a matching ring from her other jewels. I feel like she's always with me as I wear these fantastic pieces."

Touching my newly created necklace, I look toward the Heavens. I swear the lights flickered. Twice.

She was protecting me then and even now I feel she's protecting me. I smile as I look upward. "Thanks, Grandma. Rest in peace." I raise a toast with my wine glass as Shadow looks up and meows.

About the Author

WENDY VANHATTEN is a published author, editor-in-chief for "Prime Time Living Magazine," wine, food, and travel editor for "WEMagazine," and travel enthusiast. She has taught writing at the college level, writing workshops, and is affiliated with Bay Area Travel Writer Organization, http://www.batw.org/.

Her children's books, the *Max and Myron* series, teach children to read while developing good character traits.

Travel advice and photos are updated weekly on her blog at www.travelsandescapes.blogspot.com. Her books are available online at Amazon or from her website, www.wendyvanhatten.com.

Additional Titles by Wendy VanHatten

My Life, The Sequel: A Girlfriend's Guide to Personal Success

When the Cat Speaks . . . Listen: A purr . . . fectly good way to enjoy life

Dad's Hidden Box

HIDDEN TRUTHS SERIES
Champagne Lies
Vineyard Secrets

MAX & MYRON SERIES
by Wendy VanHatten and R David Kryder with illustrations by Corie Barloggi
 Max and Myron Learn Please and Thank You Max and
 Myron, My First Day of School
 Max and Myron I'm Sorry, Please Forgive Me Max & Myron
 Learn Please Don't Tease
 Max & Myron Learn Big and Small, Short and Tall

The Authorship Journey: A profitable adventure?
by Wendy Vanhatten, Ginger Marks, Misty Taggart, and Tracee Gleichner

Available on Amazon.com and fine bookstores everywhere.

www.ingramcontent.com/pod-product-compliance
Lightning Source LLC
Chambersburg PA
CBHW050427260626
47156CB00003B/1187